CW00471772

Lorenzo and Oonalaska

JOSEPH ROCCHIETTI

Edited with an Introduction and Notes by
Leonardo Buonomo

CASA LAGO PRESS
NEW FAIRFIELD, CT

Spuntini
Volume 2

This book series is dedicated to publishing studies and creative works that are longer than the traditional journal-length submission and yet shorter than the traditional book-length manuscript. It is similar to a light meal, a snack of sorts that holds you over for the full helping that comes with either lunch or dinner.

COVER ART: Léon Cogniet, "Self-portrait"
             Oil on canvas, 1817-1818
             Musée des Beaux-Arts d'Orléans

ISBN 978-1-955995-01-6
Library of Congress Control Number: Available upon request

© 2022 Leonardo Buonomo, "Introduction"
© 2022 Casa Lago Press
All rights reserved
Printed in the United States of America

CASA LAGO PRESS
New Fairfield, CT

TABLE OF CONTENTS

ACKNOWLEDGEMENTS

I am deeply grateful to Anthony Tamburri for his encouragement and guidance in the preparation of this volume. I have also benefited greatly from the advice and comments of my dear friend Gabrielle Barfoot.

A Note on the Text

In the absence of a manuscript, the text of this edition follows that of the first edition, printed in Winchester, Virginia, in 1835, by Brooks & Conrad. While a few minor emendations have been made, the original edition has been kept as intact as possible.

INTRODUCTION

Currently regarded as the earliest Italian American novel, Joseph Rocchietti's *Lorenzo and Oonalaska*, published in 1835, offers compelling evidence that the history of Italian American literature is longer, and much more varied and complex than was previously believed.[1] Before Rocchietti's novel was rediscovered at the beginning of the twenty-first century, the prevailing view among scholars of the Italian diaspora in the United States was that the earliest examples of Italian American writing, in the period preceding the 1880-1920 mass immigration wave, came primarily in the form of letters, journals, travelogues, poetry, and autobiographies. The origins of Italian American fiction were commonly believed to date back to the publication, in 1885, of Luigi Donato Ventura's novella *Peppino*, probably written in Italian and almost immediately translated into French and English (Marazzi 29-46). Presenting her retrieval of Rocchietti's long-forgotten novel in 2000, Carol Bonomo Albright appropriately drew attention to its date of publication, which seemed all the more extraordinary when placed in the context of canonical American literary history. Less than two decades separate *Lorenzo and Oonalaska* from *Precaution* (1820), the debut novel of one of the founders

---

[1] This introduction is based, in part, on my article "Alle origini della letteratura italoamericana: Joseph Rocchietti," which was published in the Fall/Winter issue, vol. 13, of the journal *Ácoma*, entitled *Riflessi di un'America italiana. Studi sulla cultura italoamericana negli Stati Uniti*, edited by Elisa Bordin and Roberto Cagliero. I am grateful to the editors of *Ácoma* for permission to reproduce, in somewhat revised form and in English, some portions of my article.

of United States fiction, James Fenimore Cooper (129). No less remarkable, in my view, is the even shorter span of time that separates *Lorenzo and Oonalaska* from the first edition of Italy's "national" novel, namely Alessandro Manzoni's *The Betrothed* (1827), which Rocchietti quotes towards the end of his novel.

Published in English by an author who had emigrated from Italy to the United States only five years earlier, *Lorenzo and Oonalaska* came out in a period in which both countries, albeit under very different circumstances, were deeply engaged in the construction of a national culture, a process in which literature was expected to play a significant role. In the United States, the search for distinctive national traits found expression in an unprecedented flowering of literature starting in the 1820s, but also in a growing identification with whiteness and, specifically, Anglo-Saxonism, at the expense of all minorities, as evidenced by the continuing expropriation of land from Native Americans, the persistence of slavery, the War against Mexico, and the discrimination against immigrants. Admittedly, the Italians who emigrated to the United States in this period were too few and far between to constitute a visible minority, but they shared with the Irish, who reached America's shores in huge numbers following the potato famine of the 1840s, the Roman Catholic faith which many Americans regarded as incompatible with the country's democratic institutions. As Catholics and non-Anglo-Saxons, early Italian immigrants were thus aligned with that otherness that xenophobic nativist movements denounced as unassimilable into the fabric of American society.

Political exiles, missionaries, adventurers, street performers, the Italians who made their way to the United States before Italy's unification in 1861 came (or, in some cases, fled from) a country that was still fragmented and largely under despotic foreign rule. While the vast majority of Americans who visited Italy in this period were more interested in the country's historical and artistic past than its political present, and often saw Italy as a picturesque refuge from American modernity, there were a few American intellectuals who took an active interest in the Italian struggle for independence and nationhood as well as the plight of Italian political exiles in the United States. For example, Catharine Maria Sedgwick, a key figure in the history of American fiction, offered, with the help of her brothers, friendship and practical assistance to such prominent Italian exiles as Federico Confalonieri, Piero Maroncelli, Felice Foresti, Giovanni Albinola and Gaetano De Castillia (Buonomo, "Past Glories" 19-21). Highly educated and mostly of middle-class (and sometimes even aristocratic) extraction, these Italians may seem to have little in common with those who would follow in their footsteps, in much larger numbers, in the later part of the nineteenth century. However, like their successors, these exiles (or political migrants, as Donna R. Gabaccia has suggested calling them [24]), did experience acute displacement in a country that, with few exceptions, was bewildering to them in terms of language, culture,

institutions, and customs.[2] Joseph Rocchietti is an inter-
esting case study of this fascinating chapter of Italian immigration to the United States and it is to be hoped that
the renewed attention his writings have received in recent
years will lead to further investigations into a corpus of
literary testimonies that has yet to be fully explored.

The frontispiece of *Lorenzo and Oonalaska* identifies
the novel's author as Joseph Rocchietti "from Casal,"
short for Casale Monferrato, in the northern Italian region
of Piedmont. Not a great deal is known about Rocchietti's
life before he emigrated to the United States and angli-
cized his given name Giuseppe. In his landmark anthol-
ogy *Italoamericana*, Francesco Durante aptly describes
Rocchietti as a man still enveloped by an aura of mystery.
Durante does point out, however, that in 1873, the editor
of the New York Italian-language newspaper *L'Eco d'Italia*, Francesco Secchi De Casali, had mentioned Rocchietti
alongside other Italian patriots who had been forced into
political exile in the United States. Having found no mention of Rocchietti in the Turin police archives, Durante
surmises that Rocchietti might have left Italy voluntarily
as a precautionary measure, for fear of repercussions,
possibly because of his participation in, or even simply
his support for, the Piedmontese uprising of 1821 (326).
This hypothesis finds partial confirmation in a letter Rocchietti wrote to Ugo Foscolo, from Geneva, Switzerland,
on November 5, 1824. In addition to expressing his pro-

---

[2] For information on Italian political exiles, see in particular: G. Stefani's
I prigionieri dello Spielberg sulla via dell'esilio and A. Bistarelli's *Gli esuli del
Risorgimento*.

found admiration for Foscolo, as well as the wish to meet him in the near future, Rocchietti divulges some relevant information about himself and his precarious circumstances. After stating his age (twenty-five, which would set his date of birth at 1799), he mentions that following the "small revolution in Piedmont two or three years earlier," he had lost his employment as instructor of arithmetic and calligraphy in an institution because of a recently enacted law which excluded lay people from teaching. He further explains that he had left Italy, and his "poor mother in tears," four months earlier, intending to join Foscolo (himself a political exile) in England and from there embark for the United States (translation mine, 462-63). Unable to continue on his journey for lack of proper documentation and shortage of money, Rocchietti had been forced to remain in Switzerland where he hoped to support himself by giving Italian lessons (as his fictional hero Lorenzo does in the novel). In the concluding part of the letter, Rocchietti ventures to hope that Foscolo might help him find steady employment and reveals that he is an aspiring author: "I have written a tragedy, my first effort, about which I would love to have your approval, before submitting it for publication." The letter (to which, as far as we know, Foscolo never replied) is at its most poignant and disarming when Rocchietti, while reiterating his literary ambitions, admits that he might need to face facts: "I feel myself called to literature; but were I unable to do that, I have two arms with which I can toil" (translation mine, 463). These words admirably sum up the peculiar character of the Italian political diaspora, wavering uneasily between lofty aspirations and the harsh reality of economic subsistence in a foreign land.

As documented and discussed by Francesco Durante, Carol Bonomo Albright and Elvira G. Di Fabio, Rocchietti did become a published author after his arrival in the United States. *Lorenzo and Oonalaska* was followed by the Italian-language tragedy *Ifigenia* in 1842, the pamphlet *Why a National Literature Cannot Flourish in the United States of North America* in 1845 and the play *Charles Rovellini* in 1875. A major contribution to our knowledge of Rocchietti's life in the United States has come from the research work that Raymond Niro presented in a 2009 article appropriately entitled "In Search of Joseph Rocchietti." Thanks to Niro's findings, we know that Rocchietti embarked for the United States in 1829 in Havre de Grâce, France, on the American ship *Charles Carroll* and landed in New York City on January 9, 1830. While the passenger manifest suggests that Rocchietti, listed as a "Professor of Languages, age thirty" was in better circumstances at the time of his voyage (he travelled in first class alongside only twelve other professional men), his early years on American soil seem to have been characterized by precariousness and instability (Niro 23-24). Regardless of the extent to which *Lorenzo and Oonalaska* accurately reflects Rocchietti's own experience, it does reveal an overwhelming preoccupation with poverty. Moreover, in his 1845 pamphlet, thinking back to his beginnings in the United States, Rocchietti complains bitterly about the discrimination, marginalization and penury he had suffered as a stranger in a strange land. He certainly moved about a great deal in search of employment. After working at the school of General Lallemand in New York, he moved to Virginia where *Lorenzo and Oonalaska* was published. Tax records retrieved by Niro show that Rocchietti either owned or rented a slave while living there, a piece of information which stands in glaring contradiction to the emphatic commitment to individual freedom permeating his novel. As Niro points out, ten years later, in the pamphlet, Rocchietti tells the story of how one day, in Virginia, he had prevented, savior-like, the summary execution of an elderly black man suspected of being an escaped slave (Niro 23-25). However, while drawing attention to the cruelty of the mob towards a fellow human being, Rocchietti stops short of explicitly condemning the institution of slavery (*Why a National Literature* 29).

In 1838 Rocchietti lived in Columbia, South Carolina, where he taught Italian and French at the Columbia Female Academy. From there he likely moved to Philadelphia, judging from the advertisement, in local papers, of his novel. By 1842 he was back in New York where he advertised his services as instructor in Italian, French, and guitar (Niro 24-26). That same year, the New York *Albion* praised *Lorenzo and Oonalaska* and mentioned that its author was "at present an able teacher of Italian in this city" (11). In April, 1845, the *New York Herald* announced the publication of *Why a National Literature Cannot Flourish in the United States of North America*. The following year, Rocchietti purchased land in the town of Rahway, New Jersey, not far from Manhattan. In the 1850 census Rocchietti was listed as a farmer. Around 1856 he married an Irish immigrant, Jane Steward (or Stewart) and they had five children. Interestingly, in his 1845 pamphlet Rocchietti had expressed his solidarity with the Irish in the United States, in a period of intense discrimination against that community, fueled largely by widespread and rabid anti-Catholicism. While we do not know the date on which Rocchietti became an American citizen, we can assume he was naturalized by 1858 when he was able to act as a witness in support of the naturalization of one Joachim Zender (Niro 27).

In the introduction to his play *Charles Rovellini*, set during the Civil War, Rocchietti laments the untimely death of two of his children, Charles and John, and appears to imply, by dedicating the play to their memory and condemning the Civil War, that they had died on the battlefield. However, as Niro has noted, the dates of birth of two of Rocchietti's sons, both named Charles—1858 and 1867—excludes the possibility that either of them participated in the conflict. Of a son named John there is no trace but he may have died in infancy and, as was not uncommon at the time, his parents may have deemed it unnecessary to register his demise. Rocchietti died of old age in Linden, New Jersey, on April 23, 1879 (Niro 28-30). Sadly, the obituary published in the *Rahway Weekly Advocate and Times* made no mention of his work as a teacher, nor of his publications.

Given Rocchietti's admiration for Ugo Foscolo, and his desire to emulate him, it comes as no surprise that for his first (and apparently only) effort as a novelist, he took inspiration from what was regarded as the preeminent

Italian example of the epistolary novel genre, namely Foscolo's *Ultime lettere di Jacopo Ortis* (*Last Letters of Jacopo Ortis*, 1802). Like Foscolo, Rocchietti paints a posthumous portrait of a quintessentially romantic hero and infuses his story with fervent patriotism as well as with a powerful denunciation of despotism and injustice. In *Lorenzo and Oonalaska*, Rocchietti simultaneously acknowledges and conceals his literary debt to Foscolo. On the one hand, he calls his hero Lorenzo, like Jacopo's friend and correspondent in *Ortis*, and includes in the frontispiece of his novel the same lines from Dante's *Purgatory* (Canto 1) that precede Jacopo's first letter in the 1816 edition of *Ortis* (Foscolo 295n1). On the other hand, he conspicuously omits any direct reference to, or quotation from, Foscolo in a novel that boasts a rich intertextual repertoire of epigraphs and citations. And while Rocchietti follows Foscolo's basic storytelling model, by alternating between the transcription of letters and the interventions of the narrator, he also departs from that format. He does so by reconstructing Lorenzo's life not only through his letters to his friend Charles and his beloved Oonalaska, but also through their replies. In addition, Rocchietti gives us access to the correspondence between Lorenzo and other characters (such as his sisters, his brother Hippolitus, and his friend Garneri), as well as to the letters that other characters exchange between themselves. It is also worth noting that, unlike Foscolo's Lorenzo, Rocchietti's narrator (and custodian of the protagonist's letters) is never identified by name.

Through the different sources to which we are made privy, Rocchietti composes the biography of a young man whose most distinctive traits are a profound intolerance of injustice, a hatred of tyranny, and, especially, a propensity to defend the weak which he displays since his early years. Significantly, the narrator opens his account by recalling two occasions on which Lorenzo jumps into action to protect schoolmates who had been targeted by bullies (one of whom, Hugo, will grow up to become Lorenzo's mortal enemy). Clearly, these episodes possess a strong exemplary quality and are intended to foreshadow the man Lorenzo will become. In particular, they show how Lorenzo, in his willingness to put himself at risk to protect friends in peril, has taken to heart the lesson imparted by his mother, namely that he should always "avoid all kind of selfishness" (5). Indeed, Rocchietti makes it clear that Lorenzo has been shaped primarily by his mother. She holds him to a higher moral standard than his father does. While the latter evaluates Lorenzo's conduct in terms of duty (hence partially excusing his use of physical violence), his mother exhorts him to strive to follow Christ's teaching and renounce violence altogether even in the presence of persecution. And this is precisely what Lorenzo will do at the end of the novel when confronted once again by his old foe Hugo, a line of conduct that will cost him his life.

Pervaded by a profound pessimism about human nature, Rocchietti's novel suggests from the outset that the very qualities that make Lorenzo stand out ("benevolence, courage, patience, fortitude in adversity, understanding, imagination, sensibility, and manly and commanding presence"), accompanied as they are by "a true spirit of liberty" (8), are simultaneously a blessing and a curse. While they win him the devotion and esteem of loyal friends and, eventually, the love of the heroine, they also make him the recipient of envy and a perpetual outsider. Betraying its autobiographical source, *Lorenzo and Oonalaska* is to a large extent a novel about displacement and exile, as well as the bitter feeling of not being properly appreciated. Tellingly, in his first letter (addressed to his friend Charles), Lorenzo shows himself painfully aware that his love of liberty ("I wanted nothing but the rights of man" [8]) puts him in grave danger and leaves him no choice but to depart from Italy at the insistence of his mother and sisters. The death of his father on the battlefield, and the execution of his brother Henry (presumably for participating in the insurrection) leave him in no doubt that if he stays his own lot will be either imprisonment or death. While historical references in the novel are few and rather vague, Lorenzo's first letter does allude obliquely to Prince Charles Albert of Savoy ("The Prince C.") who, after reneging on his initial support for the Piedmont insurrection of 1821, had further consolidated his commitment to the ancient regime by going to Spain (in 1823) to help in the effort to restore King Ferdinand VII's absolute power. Thus, Rocchietti places the story in a period in which liberal enthusiasm had been summarily quenched and Italy seemed to be firmly in the grip of despotism, both local and foreign ("Austria invades Italy" [8]). As the novel's dedication proclaims

("To Italy the misfortunes of Lorenzo are inscribed"), the protagonist's predicament is indeed closely linked to that of a country where, as Lorenzo puts it, "the sound of liberty… is now silent" (8).

The reference (however veiled) to Charles Albert also introduces a strong anti-aristocratic and anti-upper-class sentiment which reverberates throughout the novel. Just as Italian patriots, fighting for their country's independence and nationhood in the early nineteenth-century, were repeatedly disappointed and betrayed by the ruling elites, so too is Lorenzo made the victim of social disdain for his economic circumstances and envy for his moral superiority. Tellingly, Rocchietti inaugurates the account of Lorenzo's exile with an anecdote that seems designed to put the upper classes to shame. On his way to Switzerland, Lorenzo is intercepted by bandits while crossing the mountains of Savoy, but they refrain from robbing him when one of them recognizes Lorenzo as someone who has fought valiantly for the rights of the people. As the rest of the novel plainly shows, the outlaws have a better understanding and appreciation of Lorenzo's worth than most of the upper-class people with whom he comes into contact.

After struggling to make ends meet in Switzerland, Lorenzo's growing reputation as a teacher enables him to send money to his mother and sisters. However, he soon grows restless—a tendency that will punctuate his entire life—and finds himself unable to enjoy whatever comforts he has secured because he feels called upon to defend the cause of justice and liberty. Lorenzo's credentials as a Romantic hero are thus firmly established when he sets off for Missolonghi to volunteer for the Greek War of Independence, carrying a letter of introduction to real-life Greek patriot Markos Botsaris. This chapter of Lorenzo's life also aligns him with one of the most influential figures of European Romanticism, Lord Byron, and with Santorre di Santarosa, a leading figure of the Italian Risorgimento, both of whom died in Greece. An additional link between Lorenzo and Santarosa is provided by the latter's very prominent role in the Piedmonte uprising of 1821, prior to his departure for Greece. The subject of two poems included in the novel and attributed to Lorenzo, Santarosa is celebrated as the epitome of Italian virtue (as well as a role model for the protagonist) and the embodiment of bravery and selflessness.

It is the novel's heroine, a young Englishwoman with the improbable name Oonalaska Ethelbert, who brings out the poet in Lorenzo, asking him at various times during the novel to pen lines on subjects of her choice. Lorenzo meets her in Switzerland where she is staying with her parents and soon their initial relationship of teacher and pupil evolves into love. It is likely that Rocchietti took the name Oonalaska from a line in *The Pleasures of Hope* (1799) by Scottish poet Thomas Campbell ("The wolf's long howl from Oonalaska's shore" [5]). In the early nineteenth century, Campbell's poem was widely anthologized and it is possible Rocchietti may have come across it in one of the textbooks he used to learn English. It may seem odd, on Rocchietti's part, to have chosen for his English heroine a Native American place name which evoked one of the remotest and wildest corners of North America. The geographical and cultural associations of that name appear particularly incongruous with the way in which the young woman who bears it is portrayed in the novel. Although rather tenuously sketched, Oonalaska Ethelbert comes across as a typical Old World upper-class, refined young woman who, in line with prevailing nineteenth-century notions of feminine accomplishment, studies foreign languages, reads poetry, plays the harp and sings. However, the name Oonalaska may have been intended, at least in part, to suggest that the heroine represents to Lorenzo an aspiration, a vision of something removed from daily experience and perhaps unattainable. This impression is reinforced by an almost complete absence of information about her physical appearance (even though this is also true of Lorenzo and the few other characters in the novel) and the fact that she plays the role of muse to the man she loves. Indeed, except for a brief "rapturous moment of interchanged looks" (34), there is scarcely any hint of physical attraction in her relationship with Lorenzo. Theirs is essentially a meeting of minds and sensitivities. And while Lorenzo is the creative force in the relationship, she is the catalyst for his creativity and his attraction for her appears to be primarily of an intellectual nature. Articulate and extremely well-read, Oonalaska would not be out of place in a tale by Edgar Allan Poe, an author with whom, as we shall see, Rocchietti's writing is curiously connected.

In line with his portrayal of Oonalaska and his enlightened take on gender relations, Rocchietti has Lorenzo refer to the subjection of women in the Ottoman empire as one of the most blatant expressions of despotism and the pernicious effects of religion (tellingly, Lorenzo follows these reflections with a quotation from Lucretius' *De rerum natura*). While Lorenzo is especially critical of what he refers to as "the creed of Mahomet" (13), he also voices on numerous occasions his reservations on organized religion within the Christian world, primarily on the grounds of its traditional alliance with repressive governments. In addition, on the question of women's rights, Rocchietti makes clear that even in Europe, especially among the higher circles of society, women are not free agents, especially when it comes to marriage. Even though Oonalaska has clearly received a liberal education, her father sees her as a reflection and a product of his social status. He makes this very clear when he informs Lorenzo that he can have his consent to marry his daughter, as well as his help in gaining an eminent position in English society, only if he renounces his political ideas. His view of society, from the vantage point of wealth and privilege, is profoundly hierarchical and consequently irreconcilable with Lorenzo's belief in social justice and widespread access to education. Needless to say, Lorenzo cannot accept Mr. Ethelbert's terms because doing so would mean compromising his moral integrity. For the same reason, he rejects Oonalaska's proposal that they elope and persuades her to accept their forced separation. Significantly, upon refusing Mr. Ethelbert's condition (and with it, the lure of economic prosperity), Lorenzo mentions that he had solemnly sworn to his late father never to abandon the political principles embodied by "Brutus, Cato, and Washington" (37). Evoked as a name that signifies opposition to tyranny, Washington foreshadows the next chapter in Lorenzo's life, namely his emigration to the United States. Earlier in the novel, Lorenzo had also mentioned Benjamin Franklin as a term of comparison to emphasize the potential for public good of his friend and fellow exile Garneri. It is almost as if the two founding fathers of the United States joined Lorenzo's father as exemplary figures in opposition to the retrograde defense of rank and class privilege voiced by Oonalaska's father. The names of Franklin and Washington are intended to evoke the democratic and republican ideals of the United States, a nation that had come into being by overturning a foreign oppressor, thus setting an example that was particularly resonant in the early phase of the Italian Risorgimento. Interestingly enough, the course of Lorenzo's American adventure seems to parallel the gradual change in attitude towards the United States that took place among Italian intellectuals in the first half of the nineteenth century. Writing to Oonalaska from Havre, before his departure for America, Lorenzo bitterly laments the treatment of guests at the hotel where he is staying as an example of money-based social structuring. With the placement of guests and the attitude of the landlord toward them directly dependent on the depth of the former's purse, the hotel is a synecdoche of societies founded on economic discrimination. Thinking of his imminent voyage, Lorenzo alludes to his move to the New World as possibly his last chance of finding "better people" (75), that is to say those living in a more just and egalitarian society. Although couched in hypothetical form, Lorenzo's musings about America seem to echo the opinion of those Italian liberals who, as Paola Gemme has argued, in the first two decades of the nineteenth century "did look at the United States as the one democracy that had not been destroyed by the forces of reaction" (31). On the other hand, Lorenzo's subsequent disillusion (together with his decision to return to Europe) aligns him with the growing critique of American democracy, among both moderate and radical Italian liberals, which started to emerge in the 1830s. During the very period in which Rocchietti was building a new life in the United States, Italian liberals were increasingly finding fault with the American model. While moderates believed that the United States was veering dangerously towards populism, radicals thought it had abandoned its original democratic principles, and many, across ideological lines, were horrified by the institution of slavery (Gemme 31).

Interestingly, Rocchietti withholds information about Lorenzo's voyage, his landing, and his early days in the United States. By having the narrator surmise that some letters of Lorenzo's appear to have been lost, Rocchietti effectively de-mythicizes the immigrant experience. There is no reference to living conditions aboard the vessel or to the weather during the ocean crossing. Conspicuously absent is also one of the most traditional topoi of immigrant writing: the first sighting of the New World. Nor is there any mention of how Lorenzo dealt with practical matters upon arrival, such as finding lodgings, or even

what he experienced in his first hours in utterly un-
familiar surroundings. Indeed, throughout the American
section of *Lorenzo and Oonalaska* the landscape in which
the protagonist moves remains virtually invisible. We
could be anywhere or nowhere. It as if, by preventing us
from getting our bearings, Rocchietti had attempted to
convey primarily Lorenzo's (and perhaps his own) overwhelming sense of displacement. Even though the same
observation could be made about other locations in the
novel, the near-complete absence of any description of the
United States seems particularly conspicuous at a time
when, in Europe, there was a great deal of curiosity
among the reading public about the New World. Rocchietti must have sensed that this omission was particularly glaring because he felt the need to justify it in the
novel. Significantly, in his first American letter to Oonalaska (who functions here as the fictional representative of
the European reading public), Lorenzo apologizes for not
writing about "the manners and customs of this nation,"
or the beauty of nature (except for a rather vague reference to "fine mountains"), claiming that the thought of
his beloved obscures everything else before him (78).
Philadelphia, the first American city from which Lorenzo
sends his letters, is thus exclusively evoked through the
name of Benjamin Franklin whom Rocchietti, like many
Europeans at the time, seem to have regarded as the quin-
tessential American together with George Washington. In
a letter to his brother Hippolitus, Lorenzo quotes a passage from Franklin's autobiography and it is almost as if
Franklin's words served to locate the sender in a context

that otherwise would have remained utterly undistin-
guishable. Given the fortune of Franklin's autobiography,
this quotation is not surprising but it does stand out in a
novel in which the near totality of literary references
comes from European sources.

In the same letter, Lorenzo launches into a digression
on the meaning and the use of the word "Yankee." Like
the quotation from Franklin, this disquisition seems intended to compensate, at least in part, for the absence of
geographical and sociological details. In this case, a single
word serves to create the semblance of an American context. Indeed, the explanation Lorenzo provides for the
origin of the word "Yankee" takes us back to the very "beginnings" of American history—as conceived by white
Americans and Europeans—namely the first encounter
between America's indigenous populations and English
settlers. Assuming a didactic tone, Lorenzo explains that,
according to the "American dictionary," "Yankee" is the
sound that Native Americans uttered when they tried to
pronounce the word "English" (83). He then notes how
over the years it had become an incredibly adaptable dis-
paraging term that speakers would wield to assert their
superiority over those they perceived as Other, as the situation demanded. What is worth noting here is not so
much that Rocchietti, through Lorenzo, unhesitatingly
subscribes to a dubious theory, but rather that he focuses
his interest on the way in which words could be weapon-
ized to strengthen and differentiate one's identity and
culture. This is particularly evident, Lorenzo notes, when
Americans (read Anglo-Saxons) assert their sense of be-

longing and entitlement by calling "Yankees the strangers coming into America," failing to realize that the same term might well be applied to themselves, "since the American blood is stranger to this country" (84). Several decades before Italian immigrants to the United States would be forced to contend with words such as "dago" and "wop," Rocchietti seems to have grasped the tremendous power of language, when deployed by the dominant culture, to identify those who supposedly belonged in the United States and those who did not.

In Rocchietti's view, the most effective remedy against discrimination and prejudice was education, because it was naturally conducive to cosmopolitanism and a general attitude of openness and curiosity towards the world as a whole. Tellingly, Rocchietti would emphasize the need for cosmopolitanism even more emphatically ten years later in his pamphlet, during the height of Nativism in the United States.[3] In the novel, Lorenzo, an educator and a poet who is well versed in foreign languages and literatures, is the very embodiment of cosmopolitanism. Significantly, this does not diminish, but rather elevates his fervent patriotism because it prevents it from ever degenerating into chauvinism and xenophobia. This is particularly evident in a letter in which Lorenzo, writing from New York to his friend Charles, reports a conversation he had with a French lady. The latter's belief in the superiority of all things French, voiced unguardedly under the mistaken impression that her interlocutor was

---

[3] On the anti-nativist motif in Rocchietti's pamphlet, see Carol Bonomo Albright's "Joseph Rocchietti: Political Thinker in Literary Clothing."

a compatriot, is clearly intended to throw Lorenzo's cosmopolitanism into bold relief. To her "outrageous" praises of her own country, Lorenzo opposes his conviction that we "cannot find a single nation which is not adorned by men of virtue" (88).

A subsequent letter Lorenzo writes to Oonalaska from New York stands out in the American section of the novel, because it contains a rare topographic detail which allows us to place the protagonist in a recognizable urban setting. While Philadelphia and Richmond remain essentially invisible, New York comes into view, to some degree, when Lorenzo mentions a tragic event he witnessed in Maiden Lane, in the heart of the financial district, not far from Wall Street. The fact that Rocchietti chose to single out this particular location among the many that, presumably, passed before Lorenzo's eyes during his American sojourn, suggests that New York's financial district is meant to be representative of the whole nation. There, one could find a glaring display of what Rocchietti believed to be the greatest threat to American democracy and republicanism: the primacy of money over everything else. While Lorenzo calls the United States "the most promising" country in the world, he notes that it needs "better administration" (98), as a corrective, one assumes, to a system of laissez-faire and brutal economic competition. In a society with little or no regulation and protection for the vulnerable, the consequences can be tragic, as Lorenzo witnesses with his own eyes when, following "a track of blood," he comes upon the lifeless body of a merchant "who cut his throat, when he found himself failed in his business" (98). It is worth noticing that Rocchietti who, ten years later, would decry the sensationalism of the American press, here has recourse to the language of city journalism. He does so—conspicuously within a novel wherein disquisitions on ethics, literature, philosophy, religion, and politics dominate over plot and characterization—to exemplify what he regarded as the gravest malady of American society: "too much anxiety of money" (100). For Rocchietti, the only cure against this destructive obsession was, once again, education, by which he meant the study of the classical and European heritage about whose primacy he entertained no doubt whatsoever. An unapologetic Eurocentric intellectual, Rocchietti cast the United States in the role of a promising but still rough-around-the-edges pupil, in great need of instruction and refinement which an educated European such as himself was more than qualified to provide.

Through the narrator we learn that Lorenzo's brief and relatively uneventful American interlude is followed by unspecified worldwide roaming—in line with his Romantic restlessness—before his return to Switzerland. There, he finds himself once again the target of malicious gossip and envy and he is ultimately provoked to engage in a duel against his old childhood foe Hugo, after the latter had slandered Oonalaska's father. Although Lorenzo, unlike his literary model Jacopo Ortis, does not take his own life, the manner of his death is not far removed from a suicide. In his last letter to Charles, who acts as his second in the duel, Lorenzo states that he has already loaded his pistol and Charles, apparently, takes his word for it. Whether the weapon is *actually* loaded or not is open to speculation, but what is certain is that Lorenzo, in the close-range duel that follows, does not fire his pistol. Although it is Hugo who fires the fatal shot that kills him, it is Lorenzo who practically ensures his own demise. Earlier in the novel, faced with the prospect of a definitive physical separation from Oonalaska and his native country, Lorenzo had indeed contemplated suicide. His quasi-suicide at the end is configured as the ultimate noble and selfless act, because motivated by his determination not to kill another human being (in line with his mother's teachings). As the supreme form of self-sacrifice, Lorenzo's death confirms his status as a hero, aligning him with the historical figure of Cato, celebrated in the lines from Dante's *Purgatory* on the novel's frontispiece and evoked by Lorenzo as his role model. Fittingly, Oonalaska, upon learning of Lorenzo's death, joins him as a tragic heroine, by going mad and dying of a broken heart.

One of the unsolved mysteries of Rocchietti's literary production is the notable difference in English language proficiency between *Lorenzo and Oonalaska* and the pamphlet *Why a National Literature Cannot Flourish in the United States of North America*, published ten years later. While the language of the novel is often stilted and artificial, and frequently dotted with errors, its overall quality is certainly superior to what Edgar Allan Poe, in his review of the pamphlet, mercilessly described as Rocchietti's "broken English" (83). It seems odd that after ten years in the United States, Rocchietti's competence in English should have deteriorated so dramatically instead of improving, as it would be reasonable to expect. A plausible (albeit purely speculative) explanation might be that Rocchietti received some help while preparing the manuscript of the novel for publication. It is also within the realms of possibility that the novel was originally written in Italian and subsequently translated into English. Parts of the novel do sound as almost literal translations from the Italian. Interestingly, a brief notice which appeared in the *Virginia Free Press* on 6 August 1835 stated that the "singularity of a work being written in English by an Italian, will cause this book to be sought after with much avidity" and, at the same time, appealed for the indulgence of readers, acknowledging that "occasional forms of expression … are more consonant to the structure of the Italian language than to that of our own." Given the relatively meager space that Rocchietti devotes to Lorenzo's American sojourn and the vagueness of the setting in that section, he may have written most of the novel before he emigrated to the United States and added the American interlude subsequently. That would bring the composition of the novel closer to Rocchietti's appeal to Ugo Foscolo, in the letter mentioned earlier, wherein Rocchietti had addressed the Italian author as the "soul of Italy" and "the greatest man on earth whose writings chain me to virtue," thus acknowledging him as his role model (translation mine, 462). Between *Lorenzo and Oonalaska* and the pamphlet Rocchietti published the tragedy *Ifigenia* in Italian, ostensibly to use it as a textbook for his students, and this might very well be the tragedy he mentioned in his letter to Foscolo. By the time Rocchietti published the play *Charles Rovellini*, he had been living in the United States for 45 years and his mastery of English had certainly made considerable strides.

While Rocchietti may have initially struggled with the English language, his choice of the title *Why a National Literature Cannot Flourish in the United States of North America* for his pamphlet suggests that he was keenly aware of the cultural climate of the United States in the mid-nineteenth century. He seems to have known that those words were bound to touch a nerve at a time when literature was widely seen as a crucial factor in the construction of a national identity and the assertion of cultural independence from Europe. As Poe was quick to notice, the title of the pamphlet was utterly misleading, given that out of ten chapters only two deal tangentially with the alleged topic, by touching on the American theatre (but without mentioning a single American author) and the need for an international copyright law. Interestingly, Poe was not the only reader who was hooked by Rocchietti's tantalizingly provocative title. While Rocchietti was virtually unknown among Italian American Studies scholars before his rediscovery in 2000, his name makes sporadic but significant appearances in a number of "mainstream" publications devoted to the literary history of the United States, and all because of his pamphlet. For example, in 1935, the eminent American literary scholar Fred Lewis Pattee included a quick nod to Rocchietti's pamphlet in *The First Century of American literature, 1770-1870* (455). The following year, we find Rocchietti mentioned, alongside Poe and Transcendentalist author, translator and music critic John Sullivan Dwight, in an article titled "A National Literature, 1837-1855" which Benjamin T. Spencer published in the prestigious journal *American Literature* (147-48). Also worth noting is the reference to Rocchietti, alongside South Carolina novelist William Gilmore Simms (representing, respectively, northern and southern critiques of the state of American letters) in Howard Mumford Jones's 1948 *The Theory of American Literature* (89). Finally, additional evidence of the resonance of Rocchietti's pamphlet (or rather, its title) is its inclusion, in 1948, in the bibliography of the monumental *Literary History of the United States* (3: 48), edited by Robert Spiller, Willard Thorp et al, which would remain the standard literary history of the country for many years to come.

BIBLIOGRAPHY

Albright, Carol Bonomo. "Earliest Italian American Novel: *Lorenzo and Oonalaska* by Joseph Rocchietti in Virginia, 1835." *Italian Americana*, vol. 18, no. 2, Summer 2000, pp. 129-32.

Albright, Carol Bonomo. "Joseph Rocchietti: Political Thinker in Literary Clothing." *Italian Americana*, vol. 19, no. 2, Summer 2001, pp. 142-45.

Albright, Carol Bonomo, and Elvira G. Di Fabio. "Earliest Known Italian American Novelist, Essayist, and Playwright: Joseph Rocchietti." *Lit: Literature Interpretation Theory*, vol. 13, no. 3, 2002, pp. 225-48.

Albright, Carol Bonomo, and Elvira G. Di Fabio. Introduction. *Republican Ideals in the Selected Literary Works of Italian-American Joseph Rocchietti, 1835/1845*, edited by Carol Bonomo Albright and Elvira G. Di Fabio, Lewinston, NY, The Edwin Mellen Press, 2004, pp. 1-42.

Bistarelli, Agostino. *Gli esuli del Risorgimento*. Bologna, Il Mulino, 2011.

Buonomo, Leonardo. "Alle origini della letteratura italoamericana: Joseph Rocchietti." *Riflessi di un'America italiana. Studi sulla cultura italoamericana negli Stati Uniti*, a cura di Elisa Bordin e Roberto Cagliero, *Ácoma*, vol. 13, Autunno-Inverno 2017, pp. 29-45.

Buonomo, Leonardo. "Past Glories, Present Miseries: Nationality, Politics, and Art in Catharine Maria Sedgwick's *Letters from Abroad to Kindred at Home*." *Republics and Empires: Italian and American Art in Transnational Perspective, 1840-1970*, edited by Melissa Dabakis and Paul H. D. Kaplan, Manchester, Manchester University Press, 2021, pp. 17-34.

Campbell, Joseph. *The Pleasures of Hope*. London, Sampson, Low and Son, 1855.

Durante, Francesco. "Giuseppe Rocchietti," *Italoamericana. Storia e letteratura degli italiani negli Stati Uniti 1776-1880*, a cura di Francesco Durante, Milano, Mondadori, 2001, pp. 326-30.

Foscolo. Ugo. *Ultime lettere di Jacopo Ortis*. Edizione nazionale delle opere di Ugo Foscolo, vol. 4, edizione critica a cura di Giovanni Gambarin, Firenze, Le Monnier, 1970.

Gabaccia, Donna R. "Class, Exile, and Nationalism at Home and Abroad: The Italian Risorgimento." *Italian Workers of the World: Labor Migration and the Formation of Multiethnic States*, edited by Donna R. Gabaccia and Fraser M. Ottanelli, Urbana, University of Illinois Press, 2001, pp. 21-40.

Gemme, Paola. *Domesticating Foreign Struggles: The Italian Risorgimento and Antebellum American Identity*. Athens, The University of Georgia Press, 2005.

Jones, Howard Mumford. *The Theory of American Literature*. Ithaca, Cornell University Press, 1948.

"*Lorenzo and Oonalaska*, by Joseph Rocchietti." *The Albion*, vol. 1, no. 48, 26 November 1842, p. 572, https://archive.org/details/sim_albion-a-journal-of-news-politics-and-literature_1842-11-26_1_48/page/n7/mode/2up

"*Lorenzo and Oonalaska*, by Joseph Rocchietti." *Virginia Free Press*, 6 August 1835, n. p., https://virginiachronicle.com/?a= d&d=VFP18350806.1.2&e=-------en-20--1--txt-txIN--------

Marazzi, Martino. "La lente prismatica. Vita sfuggente di L. D. Ventura e propagginazione di un testo." *Peppino il lustrascarpe*, di Luigi Donato Ventura, edizione trilingue a cura di Martino Marazzi, Milano, Franco Angeli, 2007, pp. 29-46.

Niro, Raymond. "In Search of Joseph Rocchietti." *Italian Americana*, vol. 27, no. 1, Winter 2009, pp. 23-35.

Pattee, Fred Lewis. *The First Century of American Literature, 1770-1870*. New York, D. Appleton-Century Company, 1935.

Poe, Edgar Allan. Review of *Why a National Literature Cannot Flourish in the United States of North America*, by Joseph Rocchietti. *Broadway Journal*, vol. 1, no. 6, 8 February 1845, pp. 82-83.

Rocchietti, Joseph. "A Ugo Foscolo." 5 novembre 1824, *Epistolario*, di Ugo Foscolo, vol. 9 (1822-1824), a cura di Mario Scotti, Firenze, Le Monnier, 1994, pp. 462-63.

Rocchietti, Joseph. *Charles Rovellini: A Drama of the Disunited States of North America*. New York, 1875.

Rocchietti, Joseph. *Ifigenia*. New York, 1842.

Rocchietti, Joseph. *Lorenzo and Oonalaska*. Winchester, Brooks & Conrad, 1835.

Rocchietti, Joseph. *Why a National Literature Cannot Flourish in the United States of North America*. New York, printed by J. W. Kelley, 1845.

Spencer, Benjamin T. "A National Literature, 1837-1855." *American Literature*, vol. 8, no. 2, May 1936, pp. 125-59.

Spiller, Robert, and Willard Thorp et al, editors. *The Literary History of the United States*. 4 vols, New York, The Macmillan Company, 1948-1949.

Stefani, Giuseppe. *I prigionieri dello Spielberg sulla via dell'esilio*. Udine, Del Bianco, 1963.

LORENZO

AND

OONALASKA

BY

JOSEPH ROCCHIETTI

FROM

CASAL

•

Libertà va cercando ch'è sì cara,
Come sa chi per lei vita rifiuta

DANTE

•

WINCHESTER, Va.
FROM THE PRESS OF BROOKS & CONRAD
OFFICE OF THE REPUBLICAN
1835.

COPYRIGHT SECURED ACCORDING TO LAW.

To Italy
The Misfortunes of Lorenzo
Are Inscribed.

Lorenzo and Oonalaska.

Like Cato firm, like Aristides just,
Like rigid Cincinnatus nobly poor,
A dauntless soul erect, who smiled on death.
Thompson.

We hear a great many exalting the civilization of our age; but when we compare the fine precepts which men print for the improvement of society, with the carelessness, we shall not say wickedness, which makes some men to believe it is their interest to leave those sacred books in the corners of libraries, the prey of mice and moths, we cannot help thinking, that from the history of Moses to this age, although arts and sciences have improved the physical welfare of society, our moral is inferior to that of the men of the forest. The reason of our immorality, we hope, will be explained in the course of the following short history of our hero's life; and we shall see, that men of virtue often pass amongst us, not only unnoticed and unrewarded, but, whilst society receives from them the benefit of humane instruction, she pays them with the most ungrateful acts, by slandering their characters, because, like mirrors, they have shown the faults of her face.

From his childhood Lorenzo had been instructed by his mother to avoid all kind of selfishness. As we see a plant growing majestically on a fertile land, spreading delicious fruit for all who approach it, so Lorenzo, from his childhood, gave in silence and with generosity all he had in his possession. One day, going home from school with an unsealed letter written by his teacher to his father, the latter asked Lorenzo if he knew the subject of it.

"My teacher told me it is written for a grave fault I have committed; which, being a too grievous one, thought proper to leave to your discretion the punishment I deserve."

"Did you read it?"

"No; because when once I did, you told me I must not read a letter not being directed to me."

"Well, my son, come now and read it."

It was a letter inveighing against Lorenzo with the most bitter expressions, because my little hero had broke the head of Hugo, one of the schoolboys.

"Why have you done so, Lorenzo?"

"Hugo is the stronger of three boys, who, whilst two of them were holding Charles on the ground, struck my dearest friend with a stick: I was quite neutral in their quarrel; but, seeing such an ungenerous act, I could not help springing at Hugo, so that, after many struggles, becoming in possession of his stick, I struck him on the head, and he fell senseless on the ground."

"My son, if the fact is as you say, which I do not doubt, be more moderate in defending the weaker; but you have done your duty."

"Think, father, that the poor Hugo was brought senseless on his bed, and I do not know if he will recover. Father, any punishment you may inflict on me will alleviate the pain I feel in my heart for Hugo."

The father embraced his son with tears: he, afterwards, learned with feeling, that Lorenzo had before admonished the three little tyrants not to do so against Charles, and that the two untouched antagonists had threatened him to revenge Hugo.

Once, being at a window with one of his friends, the son of a baker, larger than our little hero, flung stones at them. Lorenzo entreated him to cease; but, finding the baker's son proceeding in his work, Lorenzo went in the street and knocked him down. The mischievous boy, leaving his cap on the ground, went crying away. In about an hour a servant called Lorenzo, who was summoned by his mother to go home, where he found the baker's wife claiming the money for her son's cap.

"Mother, her son has insulted me; and if he lost his cap, it is his own fault not to have picked it up."

"My son, you might be right according to human laws, but you would have done better to follow Jesus, by bearing patiently with your persecutor. Take the box in which you put the money your father gives you when you know your lesson, and give this poor woman the value of her son's cap."

"If it is because she is poor, here is the money, which I give with all my heart; but if I had suffered him to proceed much further, he would have broke the window, and perhaps have wounded my friend or me dangerously."

Whilst the other boys were filling up their memories with Greek and Latin words, which they could not understand, Lorenzo was always putting into exertion the sound moral principles which his mother inculcated upon him, not with vain words, but with her example, from the earliest period of his understanding. One day, while his teacher was endeavoring to explain the moral of a fable of Aesop, in which it is related the author gave a cent to a boy who wilfully struck him with a stone, telling him that he would gain more, by striking a richer man, who was at that moment approaching them.

"My mother," said Lorenzo, "would not so have imposed upon his ignorance, because she would have thought such an irony, not being understood by a poor mischievous boy, could drag him into great difficulties; and, indeed, the effect was, that he lost his life on the gallows."

Lorenzo was one of those almost perfect creatures, whom, from time to time, Nature gifts with benevolence, courage, patience, fortitude in adversity, understanding, imagination, sensibility, and manly and commanding presence — gifts, when all combined with a true spirit of liberty in a society where reason cannot be understood, the possessor of it leads a very miserable life. But as the object of this book is only the edition of my esteemed, and persecuted countryman's sentiments, I do not wish to increase the volume of the following letters, which are now in my possession.

TO CHARLES.

Turin.

O terre du passé, que faire en tes collines?
Quand on a mesuré tes arcs et tes ruines,
Et fouillé quelques noms dans l'urne de la mort,
On se retourne en vain vers les vivans; tout dort,
Tout, jusqu' aux souvenirs de ton antique histoire,
Qui te feraient du moins rougir devant ta gloire!
Tout dort, et cependant l'univers est debout!

Lamartine.

The Prince C.... fled into Spain; a great many of my friends left Piedmont; Austria invades Italy; and the sound of liberty repeated every where is now silent. My mother and sisters, with tears rolling down their cheeks, wish me in Switzerland, fearing the government might cast me into prison. Indeed, if they will not doom me like G..., who lost his noble life by the hands of a vile executioner, a perpetual confinement might be my end. Now I never go out without two pistols in my pocket; but what can these avail against the strongest? I, who wanted nothing but the rights of man, and sacrificed the whole of my property for my country, am now obliged to live as an outlaw. Dear mother, dear sisters! how can I leave you, now destitute of everything? The infamous tyrants, not satisfied to see us deprived of our whole property on earth, took from your mouth your daily support. But now, what can I do? I cannot stay longer in the land of my nativity. My dear father fell on the field of honour; my brother Henry was hanged for having been another Gracchus; and my brother-in-law Jacopo, and brother Hippolitus, are now fighting in Spain for the same cause of liberty. Charles, the sorrow carved on the beautiful foreheads of my sisters is enough to make me cry like a child! How different now the house of my father! If thy soul, my worthy father, see from heaven all the calamities we are undergoing by having followed thy heavenly eloquence, alas! pray the Creator of this wicked earth to send forth the thunder of his wrath on the heads of our persecutors.

A great many are passing their lives like streams meandering in a delicious garden of smiling flowers and refreshing shades. In my past life, my existence was embittered with seeing every thing injuring my liberal education; and now, I see nothing before me but a dreadful desert.

P. S. In writing to me, address your letter to Geneva.

LORENZO.

Fearing to wound the delicacy of a respectable family, we omit all particular concerns and scraps, which would only increase our volume without purpose.

TO LORENZO.

Paris.

Et pourquoi craindre la furie
D'un injuste dominateur ?
N'est-il pas une autre patrie
Dans l'avenir consolateur ?
Ainsi, quand tout fléchit dans l'empire du monde,
    Hors la grande âme de Caton,
Immobile, il entend la tempête qui gronde,
Et tient, en méditant, l'etérnité profonde,
Un poignard d'une main, et de l'autre Platon.

Delille.

But is not the country of thy Charles open to thee? Come with me to England. The days of our sports are past, my dear Lorenzo. How often I recollect the university in which we received an education so contradictory to the iron government of thy country! Who would have believed the sentiments of Cicero, Cato, Plato, Dante, Petrarch, and Machiavel, could have made unhappy my best friend Lorenzo? I will remember all my life when thou, in reading Bruto Secondo of Alfieri, spokest with such sublime eloquence against the oppressors of thy country. I feel yet a chill. If the Italian people had been present at thy oration, thou wouldst not now be obliged to flee from thy tyrants. I receive several journals from Italy, and particularly from Milan, whose pens, being sold to the German government, have the impudence to disregard every Italian genius of liberal sentiment.

Do tell me what thou wantest. I am rich. Not only is my whole property ready for thee—my blood, my life also. I do not know thy present situation: when I think of that in which some of thy countrymen are now, I feel my hair stand straight up on my head.   **CHARLES.**

In passing through the mountains of Savoy, Lorenzo met with a band of bandits.

"Here is all my money," said Lorenzo, taking out a purse in which he had three hundred livres: it was the scanty sum his mother saved from their confiscated property. But one of those outlaws, recognizing Lorenzo, said to the others not to bereave him of that subsistence, since he had seen Lorenzo fighting for the rights of the people in those last failing struggles.

"Well," answered another fellow, "keep your money: we are taking it only from the aristocrats' pockets." "God bless you, sir," said they all; and, proceeding on their way, left Lorenzo in a thousand philosophical reflections. On arriving in Switzerland he endeavored to give lessons; but as it often occurs that man avoids man in necessity, although Lorenzo was a scholar, and an eminent teacher, he was neglected. — So Voltaire:

"Les méchans sont hardis; les sages sont timides."

For more than a year, he lived only on bread and water; but when his ability became known, he gained a great deal of money, part of which he sent to his mother and sisters; but feeling a sympathy for Greece, he went to Missolonghi with letters of recommendation to one of the heroes of that city, the worthy Botsaris.[1]

We find, among Lorenzo's papers, the following copy of a letter, which seems to have been written to one of his creditors, when he was in a most heart-breaking situation:

SIR: *Geneva.*

I have received from my family two hundred livres, which I was anxious to send you immediately, and deliver myself from your insupportable persecution; but, finding I was debtor also to a gentleman who, although he does not live so comfortably as you, never asked me for a single livre; beside, having dealt equitably with me, which you did not, I determined to follow the laws of reason, by doing at first my duty to him.—Spare your trouble in sending every week for your money, since my intention is to leave not a single sous of debt.

TO CHARLES.

Missolonghi.

La verità nelle anime corrotte è come il tuono che mugghia nelle tombe, ma non risveglia i cadaveri.   *Pananti.*

I cannot understand the Romaic; but, in general, the Italian language is tolerably well understood here. The state of Greece is in great danger; they have a great many intestine divisions: however I am determined to be either conqueror or conquered for the good cause. A man must operate according to his own sentiments. The greater part of Greece is for freedom. I shall do all a man ought to do against the tyrants of an oppressed people. And when shall we see our rights established among men? The Pope, not feeling the interest his predecessor felt in the time of the Crusades, does not impart his holy blessings in favor of his own Christianity, against the believers of Mahomet, because he prefers to sustain his temporal holiness with the diabolical alliance of kings, than to be crowned in heaven by the hand of Jesus: and now he is silent as a convict before the judges.   **LORENZO.**

TO CHARLES.

Missolonghi.

La nature appelle en vain à elle le reste des hommes; chacun d'eux se fait d'elle une image qu'il revêt de ses propres passions. Il poursuit, toute sa vie, ce vain fantôme qui l'égare, et it se plaint ensuite au ciel de J'erreur qu'il s'est formée lui-même.

Paul et Virginie.

From my window I see the Turks surrounding the city of the most brave Greeks. Will men always be in contradiction with themselves? Behold, Charles, within the walls of this city, men struggling against tyranny, and a greater number without ready to slay the former, because they took arms to defend their own rights. And for whom are those Turks now fighting against us? For the Sultan! for a man swimming in a haram of pleasures: for a man who shuts up their daughters in golden rooms, because they were the prettiest of the country: and after having shed their blood on the field, they present willingly their heads to the executioner, if the freak should pass through their master's brain of seeing their heads on the ground. And do you believe, Charles, they would be so blind, if they were not under the creed of Mahomet? So Lucretius —

"Bantum religio potuit suadere malorum."

Write to my mother to tell my sister Carlotta, not to be alarmed about my situation. From the very moment that we, poor creatures of clay, breathe the breath of life, we are doomed to make the first step towards the occident, among a thousand dangers, which very often put an end to us before the short period of 75 years of age. And, does this life of calamities deserve an attachment? My life is nothing else but a little spark, losing itself in infinity of atoms; and when the molecules will be dissipated, it shall be the same as it was, obscurity around its little circle. Before the end of it, I am told, by my dear father, to act with honor and integrity towards the sufferers: I feel his own soul in my heart: and if I have a son, I would teach him the same principles: liberty, or death. While my soul animates this frame, I will act according to my own reason: nothing is more painful for me than when I am in contradiction with myself. Nobody, I think, can have more sensibility than my sister; and I tremble for her health: she is so delicate—my tears drop on this paper! I cannot proceed writing about her. Tell my sisters I am cheerful in danger, and thoughtful in prosperity: and if I have any thing dear on earth, and which attaches me to this existence, it is knowing I am the object of the thought of our family, and the brother of my dear Carlotta.

LORENZO.

TO CHARLES.

Missolonghi.

J'erre maintenant sans patrie. Quand je ne serai plus, aucun ami ne mettra un peu d'herbe sur mon corps pour le garantir des mouches. Le corps d'un étranger malheureux n'intéresse personne.   *Chateaubriand.*

Greece is swimming in her sacred blood; and I have now very little hope of seeing her free. These annals deserve another Tacitus. Walking one day in the environs of Geneva, I met a Greek, with whom I proceeded towards

Salève. The poor old man cried like a child in relating his misfortunes. If in five months he did not pay a debt of two thousand livres to a Turk, this believer in Mahomet would become the master of his wife and children; and his daughters obliged to marry him. They were at that time in his possession. The people of that country were raising a subscription for the poor Greek. May it please God to give a perpetual enjoyment of liberty to the nation of Tell. And why do not all nations shake hands with each other, and crush to death the few tyrants of this planet? Shall we always be obliged to exclaim with Campbell—

"Shall crimes and tyrants cease but with the world?"

LORENZO.

TO CHARLES.

Missolonghi.

Ainsi, quand Galilée accusé de génie,
Subit d'une prison l'illustre ignominie,
Les juges, qu'à son joug l'ignorance attachait
Disaient: la terre est fixe ... et la terre marchait.

Bignan.

It is not to one whose idol is money; it is not to one who believes he has reached the top of reason by having become insensible to every thing; it is not to him whose friendship grows cold towards his friend when he knows his fortune has been lost, I am now writing this letter; not to an individual who feels no interest but towards his relations or happy friends, without giving a look of compassion on misfortune, from whom they have no hope of reward. I write to you, dear Charles, whose country is the globe, because every where it is inhabited by suffering beings: to you, whose religion is neither a hypocritical dress of vices, nor an intolerable ignorance and superstition. Wearied of being confined within these walls of Missolonghi, I perused to-day several books which came to my hand; and passing so my time with those men, from whom we learn to become better, I cried like a child in reading the misfortunes of their lives.

> "N'a-t-il pas expié par trois ans de prison
> L'inexcusable tort d'avoir trop tôt raison?"

The selfishness of thousands and thousands of tyrants, is not sufficient to degrade humanity, when we think that a Socrates and an Aristides were men too. When we see Mutius Scævola putting his right hand in the fire without manifesting the least symptom of pain in his countenance, we feel ourselves dignified. When I cast my eyes on the times which are passed, I feel for those geniuses who consumed their lives for the improvement of an ungrateful society who often committed them into prison, or left them dying on the straw....

LORENZO.

The heroes of Missolonghi, seeing the impossibility of defending their post, in blowing up the city buried themselves with a greater number of Turks. Lorenzo had been one of the few spared from that destruction: he went under another Greek banner, and fought during all the campaign, in which he had been wounded once in the left arm by a ball, and a second time in the left thumb by the hanger of a Turk, whom, after a long struggle, Lorenzo took prisoner. But the despotical cabinet of Europe having acted in a manner unworthy the sons of Themistocles and Leonidas, he went back into Switzerland. Knowing very little of the agitated life of our hero from the time of the insurrection in Italy, which happened in the year 1821, to the epoch he came back to Lausanne, in which country resided a great many Italian emigrants, whom, whilst Lorenzo was in Greece, the government of Switzerland had been forced to send away by order of the despotical powers surrounding that Republic, we shall only transcribe the following letters, written from the Cantons of Vaud and Geneva.

TO CHARLES.

Lausanne.

Il n'était pas difficile de voir que, s'il est impossible que dans la société tous les individus qui la composent aient le même degré de puissance et de richesses, il est pourtant juste que tous jouissent dans la même proportion de la protection de la loi civile, ce à quoi tendait effectivement l'esprit des lois romaines.   *Botta.*

I believe the elected souls do not enjoy more pleasure than I do every morning in beholding a cloudless sky. The solitude in which now I live is for me an Elysium. I will change that uncultivated land on the mountain, into a delightful Eden; I shall see the branches of those trees I have planted, loaded with fruit; and thou, dear Charles, when wearied of thy society, wilt come to pour all thy cares into my bosom, I shall shew thee from under the beech-tree, which is on the top of the hill, this fine country. The dinners I take with Bran, under the cool bower, are delightful; thou shouldst be very much pleased in seeing this extraordinary dog! It is a present of Oonalaska, a young lady from thy country…. Here, I do not see the rich paying with usury the poor who served him with the sweat of his brow. Here, I do not see a beauty, the slave of superfluities: thou mightest have all the virtues of Socrates, the strength of Hercules, and the beauty of Ganymede; if thou art not rich, thou wilt be loved by such a woman, as if thou wert an Aesop without his wit.

I do not know whether it is in being out of my father's house, or my strange position in a society I dislike; but when I was in the most miserable situation, in walking through a crowd of people, every body seemed to me without sentiment….

A superstitious veneration for Kings, spoils our understanding. Behold that nation loving the son of Alexander for no other reason than that of being the son of the conqueror of the world. Ulysses threw Astyanax from the tower, fearing the people might put him on the throne of his ancestors. History teaches us the people had always been just when the leaders were so; and when they had committed faults, it was from the influence of a deceitful man who gilded bad logic with eloquence. So that, sometimes, nations are fighting not for their common rights, they shed their blood to put on the throne the son of their King, who, as the story relates, had not only degenerated from his father's virtues, but too often became their most shocking tyrant. It seems that men like to kiss the hand which strikes them; and afterwards they become so fond of their master, that they try to demonstrate, that man is not born to live under a free constitution; and wishing to cover their shame, they endeavor to shew defects among Republics, whilst they are unaware their servitude so dimmed their eyes that they cannot see the eagle's flight.

Here I am neither obliged to speak haughtily to the

clown, nor affectionately to those of exalted birth. I may now linger on objects agreeable to me, without losing time in insignificant attentions and ceremonies which people bestow one upon another. If sad, the cheerfulness of others seems an insult to you; and if cheerful, you incur the disgust of being laughed at, by a concealed rival, who is waiting the moment of your goodness, eccentricity, or inattention, to injure you.

I find among animals something more than that which divines call a mere natural instinct to avoid pains and death. The animal feels something more than self love. We see men so much attached to the study of philosophy, becoming insensible to every thing that recoils from reason. Codrus, Curtius, Decius, and Peter Micca going willingly to certain death, the love of their country being superior to the love of themselves: a lover for his mistress, and a mother for her child: so that, we see this noble feeling more or less among animals too. Yesterday seeing a nest in a bush; and being anxious to know if the little ones would take any crumbs from my hand, I approached them, when suddenly their mother flew against my face, and with cries of lamentation pecked me with the bravery of a lion. I retired from that awful place with veneration. I brought to-day something for them to eat to the foot of that sacred bush: and I will do it hereafter, until I shall hear the cheerful notes of her reconciliation.

Take from man the love of glory, humanity is nothing but idle clay moving about, without purpose. The construction of this mysterious universe forces us to think there is a Divinity beyond our reach, inspiring us continually with the love of glory. It makes us poets or historians to eternize the deeds of our predecessors. Hence the songs of the country inspire those hearts susceptible of love with a desire to signalize themselves, by imitating their fathers' virtues: the love of ourselves creates pictures whence to represent, either the glorious battles of a generous captain, or the happy fields where industry had caused to bloom a happy age. What more? The love of ourselves creates laws, without which society would be a forest of tigresses.   **LORENZO.**

Between the above letter and the following, there is an interval of about a year, in which we know nothing of him but from rumor. We heard the aristocratical party of that country, when speaking about Lorenzo, describing him with malicious colors, whilst the poor were giving blessings to the whimsical, (so he was epitheted,) shy, brave, and generous Italian gentleman who resided at the foot of Jura. All we know with certainty, is, that Mr Ethelbert, an English gentleman, having travelled with his wife Elizabeth and daughter Oonalaska through France and Italy, stopped in Geneva for a long while, and there became acquainted with Lorenzo, who at that time taught Greek, Latin, French, and Italian. Oonalaska became one of his pupils and her father and mother were so pleased with Lorenzo's society, that they loved him as a son; so that, this English family excepted, our hero lived in seclusion from other society, meditating on the writings of Plato and Rousseau.

TO GARNERI.

Canton de Vaud.

Je le lisais partout ce nom rempli de charmes,
Et je le relisais, et je versais des larmes.
D'un éloge enchanteur toujours environné,
A mes yeux éblouis il s'offrait couronne.
Je l'écrivais... bientôt je n'osais plus l'écrire,

Et mon timide amour se changeait en sourire.
Il me cherchait la nuit, il berçait mon sommeil;
Il resonnait encore autour de mon réveil:
Il errait dans mon souffle, et lorsque je soupire
C'est lui qui me caresse et que mon cœur respire.

Mad. Desbordes.

The winter is passed: the spring smiles every where. Few books, and the warbling of birds, give me a charming existence. Yesterday morning I rowed on the Leman Lake with a fisherman. In going to my residence, which lies on the shore, the twilight was reflecting on the steady water, and the fine tale of Rousseau was passing through my imagination with lively colors: but Oonalaska was not at my side! Garneri, in reading her name, do you see, like me, every thing smiling around you? The love I feel for Oonalaska has changed this earth into a garden of heaven.

LORENZO.

TO LORENZO.

Lausanne.

Toi qui m'aimas peut-être, ou dont l'art séducteur
Par l'ombre de l'amour trompa du moins mon cœur!
Qu'importe que le tien ne fût qu'un doux mensonge?
Je fus heureux par toi; tout bonheur est un songe!

Lamartine.

Emma wrote to me. It is not a love-letter; she pities my situation, and tells me she has found a way by which I can get, with my work, a daily support. However, although she tells me I am very proud because I did not receive her money, it is a kind letter; and I may say with the "Lettres d'une Péruvienne, 'Le poids de la reconnoissance est bien léger quand on ne le reçoit que des mains de la vertu'": so that, with her magic writing folded on my bosom, the last night I was contemplating from my window the firmament of myriads of other solar systems. Mont Blanc was reflecting from the Leman, still as a mirror, the silver brightness of the moon: a river of thoughts was passing through my mind, when, hearing the clock strike four in the morning, I went to bed. Those who never enjoyed the pleasure of a smiling landscape, who never felt the heavenly sentiment at the idea of being beloved, did never exist. Our best enjoyments are those created by our imagination; and if not so, Lorenzo, I should be unhappy. Reason, which makes us patient children of our sufferings, cannot mitigate the conscious sentiment of being unnoticed by the object of our love. Although dragged like me from our country, Lorenzo, you are now not so unhappy as I: an angel leads you by the hand, feeling for you as Heloise felt for Abelard: "Nihil unquam, Deus scit, in te requisivi: te pure, non tua concupiscens. Non matrimonii fœdera, non dotes aliquas expectavi, non denique meas voluptates, aut voluntates, sed tuas sicut ipse nosti, adimplere studui." So, your fair Oonalaska. I am, Lorenzo, destitute of all your gifts of nature, and I love Emma without hope, since nature has given me a soul full of sensibility in a frame incapable to inspire in her a sentiment of love for me; and this earth without love, can it be any thing else than a vast and cold desert of warlike ravens?

GARNERI.

Garneri had so delicate a soul, that his corporal qualities were imperfect: he was one of the greatest of moralists: if he had not been obliged to leave his country for politics, Italy would have had another Franklin in him. Being daily obliged to work for his existence, he lost the best part of his time in writing ciphers on a merchant's book; but, having portrayed Emma in such lively colors, afterwards he was reputed one of the best limners of the country, and gained a great deal of money. One day, being occupied on like business, a boy entered his room, asking him a thousand pardons for having insulted him the day before on the street by asking him if he would sell his hump.

"You did not notice me," said the boy; "it seemed, sir, you were pre-occupied with some serious thoughts; and when I reached home, I heard you had just come from our house, where you had given money to my father, whom you saw surrounded by my little brothers and sisters in want."

TO LORENZO.

Bern.

God is thy law, thou mine: to know no more
Is woman's happiest knowledge, and her praise.
With thee conversing, I forget all time,
All seasons, and their change: all please alike.

Milton.

We have been in several parts of Switzerland: if I were to write you the description of every place which pleased me, I could not be able to finish this letter in a week. When we shall have returned to Geneva, I will have the pleasure to tell you every thing. I sat down on the very place where the son of William Tell was put with an apple on his head by order of Gessler. Write for me a sonnet in your fine language on this subject: I want some poetical composition from you. I found in this city a friend of yours, who gave me some of your French verses. He does not know he has given me what I most value on earth.

My father and mother send their love to their son

Lorenzo. Good-by, my dear brother: I long for the pleasure of seeing you in Geneva in a short time.   **OONALASKA.**

———————————————————

TO OONALASKA.

Geneva.

As I bent down to look, just opposite
A shape within the watery gleam appear'd,
Bending to look on me: I started back;
It started back: but pleased I soon return'd;
Pleased it return'd as soon with answering looks
Of sympathy and love: there I had fix'd
Mine eyes till now, and pined with vain desire,
Had not a voice thus warn'd me.   *Milton.*

Since you left Geneva, every pleasure is gone from me. I began a thousand things, and I finished none. Bran, the only companion of my solitude, seems to partake my despondency. A few nights ago, I caught the man who stole a great many flowers from your garden: he has been so much frightened, that I believe his promise to come no more.

GUGLIELMO TELL.

Sonetto.

Colui che veggio di soldati cinto,
    Si: Gessler egli è desso: il dice il volto
    Ebro di gioia nel veder lo stolto
    Ahi! propolo tremante in lacci avvinto.
Guglielmo e quegli: mira l'occhio tinto
    D'alto furor che serba in cor ravvolto.
    Ma quel fanciul dal biondo crine incolto,
    Or or cader vedrò nel sangue estinto?
Stilla cade sull'arco! al punto è fiso:
    D'orror silenzio regna universale,

E colle mani ognun nasconde il viso.
Mentr'esce dalla mischia irato un uomo
Per afferrar del padre il crudo strale
Fischia, la fronte lambe, invola il pomo.

LORENZO.

TO LORENZO.

Bern.

Notre cœur est un instrument incomplet, une lyre où il manque de cordes, et où nous sommes forcés de rendre les accens de la joie sur le ton consacré aux soupirs. – *Falkland.*

A heart and feelings in perfect unison with ours, are most difficult to be met with. Education and custom oblige us to suppress natural feeling, and appear in the world the thing we are not; and, if by chance, supposing ourselves friends, nature asserting her rights, we shew ourselves as we are and as we ought to be, malice and envy immediately set to work to make us every thing we are not: so defame that merit which they cannot help inwardly acknowledging, until disgusted with the world, and its littleness, we retire within ourselves, and look upon it with contempt. Miserable is that being whose heart is formed with every kind feeling towards his fellow-creatures; yet, looks around in vain for one congenial mind, into whose bosom it may pour the rich treasure of its affection: it fears to love, lest it meets with coldness and contempt: it fears to place confidence, lest it be betrayed: thus, the heart which possesses every requisite to make others happy, cannot be so in itself: its best feelings are chilled, its best affections are nipped in the bud: thus the mind, having no external object on which it can repose itself, is obliged to have recourse to those intellecttual pursuits, which can then alone render life desirable, by diverting its thoughts from its unoccupied feelings. But, there are moments, when even these pursuits, delightful as they may be, are not all-sufficient.

If, in our pilgrimage through life, we chance to find one being who seems capable of understanding us who thinks and feels as we do, to whom it is not necessary to explain our feelings, with what pleasure do we look on, and converse with that being. The soul seems to have formed its better half, unto which it expands with delight; all is instantly seen through another medium; to the heartlessness of the world we are no longer sensible; our pains are mitigated, and our pleasures heightened.

I want a true definition of the word society, Lorenzo: I believe that we abuse such a heavenly word, since we call society a great many persons crowded in a room, whilst you see among them nothing but feelings of self-interest: it seems to me that the society of snow-birds or geese are more deserving than ours, though we call ourselves reasonable creatures.

I read in the newspapers an account of your emigrate friend Santarosa.[2] I feel a great deal for him, whom I saw several times in Lausanne with others of your countrymen. Write for me a sonnet on his departure for Greece. It might be, as you say, it is my friendship which makes me feel your verses; but since for me nothing is superior, why will you not give me such enjoyment?

OONALASKA.

TO OONALASKA.

Geneva.

There is a certain string which, if properly struck, the human heart is made to answer. *Blair.*

Thy friendship is a gift which heaven sent on earth to fill me with love to men. Thy letter, Oonalaska, inspires me with a tenderness which is no stranger to my heart: the idea that thou thinkest of me, makes dear my life, mankind seems to partake of thy angelic feeling, and my soul rejoices.

You ask me to define society? Examine your heart, Oonalaska, and you will find a plain explanation of it. The following lines of the Spectator will give you a sufficient idea of a good being's influence over society: "He does not seem," says he, "to contribute any thing to the mirth of the company; and yet, upon reflection, you find it all happened by his being there." Excuse my praise; but, how can I write to you without thinking of your qualities! Examine your heart I say, and you will find you are the soul of society. It is not your fair presence which animates all who surround you: it would be a faint quality without the goodness of your heart which shines around your angelic person. Where is the man or woman who does not desire to become as kind as you? Every person in the circle of your society feels an encouragement to become better; and as they cannot do otherwise than love you, in the very moment you are their superior, they enjoy the agreeable sentiment of seeing you wishing to be no more than their equal. A sentiment quite contrary to that vulgar countenance of a great many smiling, conceited coquettes or coxcombs, who, not knowing how to do better, are continually striving to show superiority over all those who surround them. But, whilst they fatigue their society, they are doing nothing but to tire themselves; and, when getting home, believing to have been the soul of the evening party, they pass the next day in criticising those who could not take a part in such dandy fastidiousnesses.

Where are those times in which men did not clog the most noble feeling with which nature gifted humanity? Unhappy race! Ye dance at the clinking of your chains. But when, ambitious man, didst thou feel in thy heart a real pleasure amidst thy noisy fineries? Thou canst not enjoy the love for which nature created us.

> Tanto m'aggrada il tuo comandamento,
> Che l'ubbidir, se già fosse, m'è tardi.   *Dante.*

LA PARTENZA DI SANTAROSA PER LA GRECIA.
Sonetto.

Gli occhi all' Italia intenti avea il guerriero,
 E sulla fronte stavagli lo sdegno;
 Il cuore gli rodeva il destin fero,
 E di Nettuno il pin solcava il regno.
Un Genio si vedea di pianto pregno
 Volare intorno lo stendardo nero,
 Che, dal vento agitato, dava il segno
 Là guerra fa il Sultano al Dio-vero.
L'ombre di Machiavelli, Alfieri e Dante
 Scendean accompagnate da Bellona,
 E Libertà l'ali spiegava innante.
Portavan, le tre destre che vergàro
 Gli umani dritti, laurea corona,
 E a Santarosa in capo la posàro.

It is with pleasure, Oonalaska, I heard some gentle-men of Geneva wishing to blot out capital penalty from human laws. We have only to read history, and we shall find the increasing of pains had only augmented crimes when the legislators did so, without providing for the poor wretches upon whom society had turned the back. Let us give to every body the means of sustaining themselves, and then, like Alfred of England, we shall have the satisfaction of hanging golden bracelets on public roads, with the certainty that nobody would touch them. I transcribe a sonnet I wrote on this subject.

SULL'ABOLIZIONE DELLA PENA DI MORTE.
Sonetto.

Apri del santuario omai le porte;
　　Sorge una legge degna di Salone,
　　Temi, dai re negletta; in bando pone
　　Dell' uomo degradato orribil morte.
Ma se a virtude ride amica sorte,
　　Ove s'inalzi un giovane Scipione,
　　Ognuno s'incoraggi a bella azione,
　　Si frangan di miseria le ritorte:
Ove lo merto personal s'onori,
　　E non di nobil padre infame figlio;
　　Ove il lusso le vergini non sfiori:
La religion non metta iniquo artiglio
　　Di Libertà sui cari, sacri allori,
　　Diva, chi, merterà lo tuo cipiglio?

LORENZO.

TO LORENZO.

Neufchatel.

Last night I went to a ball, at which, instead of enjoying the society of each other, I found a great many strangers wanting only to show a consciousness of superiority over their fellow beings. It would seem that such aristocratic creatures go into society with no other purpose than as candidates for king and queen, to secure the favor of their inferiors. I would not give an hour of your society, Lorenzo, for all the balls of the universe. In the house we are at present, we have a company congenial to me. In a few days we shall be in Geneva, where I intend "educare la famiglia dei fiori," which you have protected from the rapacity of the nocturnal man.

OONALASKA.

TO OONALASKA.

Geneva.

Turn from the glitt'ring bribe thy scornful eye,
Nor sell for gold, what gold could never buy,
The peaceful slumber, self approving day,
Unsullied fame, and conscience ever gay.

Johnson.

ODE.

Lascia le danze, ingenua,
  Figlia de la bellezza;
  Lascia il rumor le veglie,
  Che il mondo tanto apprezza.

Aspersi d'amarissime
  Pene son tai contenti:
  Restan, passati, deboli,
  Vani sovvenimenti.

Merta piaceri stabili
  Il tuo ben fatto cuore:
  Da tuoi grand'occhi l'anima
  Uscire vidi fuore.

D'ambrosia e in un di nettare
   Sentii l'aura impregnata;
   Ed oltre l'alte nuvole
   La mia fu trasportata.

Divo piacer non abita
   Sulla terrestre mole;
   Lieve, sublime e celere
   Vola di là del Sole.

Lascia il teatro insipido
   De'grami tempi nostri:
   Non più sentir altissimo
   Echeggiar fa suoi chiostri.

Le sole note musiche
   Oman pensier snervati;
   E intanto la tirannide
   Beviam de'sciagurati.

Lascia l'amaro calice
   Che l'uomo porge all'uomo:
   Tutti quaggiù contendonsi
   Della Discordia il pomo.

Vieni negli amenissimi
   Campi de la Natura:
   Là, su que' colli liberi,
   Spirar un'aura pura.

Su rupi solitarie
   Vivremo là contenti;
   E cangieransi in giubilo
   I lunghi miei lamenti.

Al sorger de' crepuscoli
   Corrò li freschi fiori

In compagnia de'zefiri,
Di Flora e degli amori.

E mentre i sogni aleggiano
Dintorno al casto letto,
Alle tue nari eburnee
Accosterò il mazzetto

Ove fragranza diati
Sogno di paradiso,
Vedrò sul labbro, estatico,
L'almo tuo bel sorriso.

Sorgi, dirò, vivifica
La terra, il mare, il cielo:
Le rose appese al talamo
Curvan per te lo stelo.

Quindi sui campi correre,
Cinti di primavera;
Alzare i nostri cantici
Alla stellata sera:

O sotto un lauro leggere
I pianti di Malvina,
O coll' Ariosto ridere
Della rugosa Alcina.

All'ombra di que' salici
Mirar del rivo l'onda;
O sul lago ceruleo
Solcare l'altra sponda.

E mentre il giardin educa
Tua mano delicata,
Coll' incurvato vomere
Fendo la terra grata.

Sotto la fresca pergola,
   Su quel ridente prato,
   Ove gli uccelli libransi,
   Là, pranzeremo allato.

Eco farà mia cetera
   Al nobile tuo canto:
   Ti narrerò di Tacito
   La storia: Achille al Xanto.

La morte di Temistocle
   Sgorgar faratti il brio
   D'una sublime lagrima
   Che renderammi un Dio.

Così passando i labili
   Giorni di morte a strida,
   Non saran mai monotoni
   Se la virtù ci guida.,

L'uomo di senno misero
   Senz'immaginazione,
   La chiama vita insipida
   Sol dato all'ambizione.

Intento negli amabili
   Tuoi occhi indagherò
   Tutto ciò che desideri.
   Vieni, t'adorerò.

LORENZO.

Oonalaska was playing on the harp, when Lorenzo entered her room.

"Why do you not proceed, Oonalaska."

"I shall; but, after so long an absence, I want to tell you a great many things."

They sat down near a window, from whence the lake of Geneva presented a beautiful landscape.

"How fine is now that lake, Lorenzo!"

"Very much so."

"Do you see the steamboat?"

"I see it reflected in your eyes."

She smiled and blushed; and after a rapturous moment of interchanged looks, with her innocent manners, Oonalaska related all the little adventures of their voyage. Afterward she took the Vicar of Wakefield; and, in presenting it to Lorenzo, she asked if he had ever read that fine tale.

"I have, Oonalaska; but every time I open it, it seems always new to me."

"Well, Lorenzo, read it now for me, whilst I am sewing this handkerchief for my father."

He read; but the fine descriptions of that little book could not prevent our reader from stopping, when he saw a tear rolling down the cheek of Oonalaska.

"Well, Lorenzo, to-morrow we will proceed from this touching passage: for the moment I will fulfil my promise."

She took her harp, and with an expressive voice, she sung: "Di piacer mi balza il cor."[3]

The sunset was giving his last ray to the horizon of the lake of Geneva, when Lorenzo took leave of Oonalaska. In going home, which was about two miles from that of Mr Ethelbert, the full moon was enlightening the walk, which his lovely thoughts rendered still more delightful; and whilst he saw no obstacles before his future happiness, his imagination was in ecstasy. But did the sky ever shine a long time for a worthy man of this earth?

TO LORENZO.

Geneva.

Come, Lorenzo, and vivify all nature which surrounds me. You request me to scrutinize your actions, but I cannot find a single imperfection in you: my friendship cannot have blinded me, since the feeling I have towards you is grounded upon the knowledge I had of your fine qualities. Oh! teach me, Lorenzo, the means of becoming perfect; every defect you will point out to me, will confer the greatest favor on your Oonalaska, whose only desire is to become the worthy friend of Lorenzo.

Why, Lorenzo, does it happen to me, that very seldom I meet with people not wounding my feelings?

OONALASKA.

TO OONALASKA.

Nime.

Heureux qui, s'éloignant pendant que l'erreur dure,
Emporte dans son cœur une image encore pure;
Qui peut, dans les horreurs de son triste avenir,
Nourir comme un flambeau quelque cher souvenir,
Et ne voit pas du moins, en perdant ce qu'il aime,
Cette idole qui tombe ou qu'il brisa lui-même,
D'un bonheur qui n'est plus, étaler les débris
Ou l'éternel remords rampe auprès du mépris.

Lamartine.

Leave, Oonalaska, the speech of imagination: it has too great power on my mind when it comes from you: do not praise my good qualities if you find any in me. When I will do anything deserving your approbation, your silence will be enough: but, praises, flowing from lips so dear, may raise my vanity.

When we step aside from nature, that is to say, when we go a step towards society, our reason and feeling undergo sufferings at every moment. Example, Oonalaska, is so powerful, that when society has any faults, though willing to become better, we are forced to do like others, lest we should run the chance of being thought singular. A total loneliness, changes us into savages; and our sensibility, in a short time, falls into susceptibility. So Byron:

> "Alone I could not
> Nor would be happy: but, with those around us,
> I think I could be so."

Man is the only creature on earth worthy of society; still, society becomes a burthen to those, who see selfishness destroying even the enjoyments of selfishness itself. Like crowds of people, who, with eagerness press around an object of curiosity, that instead of making a large circle, throw themselves one upon another: and then, not only do they obstruct the view of those, who are behind them; but injure themselves by intercepting the light from the object of their curiosity. So, life is nothing but the anxiety of misers. Whilst nature can impart to all her children her benefits with an incredible liberality, they are doing nothing else, than losing time to agglomerate fortune to the loss of others.

When heaven sends any philanthropist on this miserable planet, to teach us we are the sons of the Almighty, such a virtuous man becomes oftener the victim of envy, because, like the sun, he brings to light the deeds that vice covets to conceal in darkness. Posterity may put him on the altar of reason; but, sometimes history is unjust, or cannot produce in evidence all generous actions which too often are stained by infernal hypocrisy. So Shakespeare: "Be

thou as chaste as ice, as pure as snow, thou shalt not escape
calumny."   **LORENZO.**

Mr Ethelbert, finding his daughter in love with Lorenzo, one day he called the latter in his private room.

"Lorenzo," said he, "Your sincerity leads me to per-
ceive your love towards my daughter. I would have no
objection if your political sentiments were like mine: however, after having been disappointed in your noble struggles, I find no reason why you should not renounce your
democracy. I am a rich man in England, and I have this
only daughter: should you coincide with me, not only
Oonalaska is your wife; but, with my means and your talents, I promise you an eminent place in London."

"Dear sir," replied Lorenzo, "I love Oonalaska, and
could not be happy had I all the world without her. But, sir,
you are not bound as I am in behalf of my sentiments towards a Republic. I admire your politeness and hospitality,
Mr Ethelbert, in not having opposed my sentiments: but
permit me only to tell you, that the cause I advocate is but
the progress of education, which will bring all nations to
banish any other government but that in favor of plurality.
But, from this moment, in paying homage to your gentility,
I will always be silent on this subject."

"No, Lorenzo, it cannot be, unless you abandon your
principles."

"It is impossible, Mr Ethelbert; a few days before my
dear father expired on the field of honour, he made me
swear against every other principle of politic but those of
Brutus, Cato, and Washington."

"It is with a breaking heart I must tell you, Lorenzo,
you cannot be my son-in-law."

It was enough for Lorenzo to understand that Mr

Ethelbert, in telling him he could not be his son-in-law, he was too polite for objecting further visits. So that, without uttering a single word to Oonalaska, with a heart-break, Lorenzo took leave from the object of all his hopes.

In going home, Lorenzo felt quite a contrary senti-ment from few evenings before: the moon was not up, and the scenery, in which love was presented so delight-fully to his hopeful imagination, was now as gloomy as his mind. After a week, a servant of Oonalaska brought him the following letter:

TO LORENZO.

Coligny.

What keeps you from me so long? I have been in-formed you are not sick. Last night, Lorenzo, I had a dread-ful dream: it seemed you were dying in my arms; when I was awaked by mother, I found myself suffused in tears. Oh, Lorenzo, a terrible presentiment threatens me; oh, re-lieve me from such a terrible situation!

OONALASKA.

TO OONALASKA.

Geneva.

We are not born for happiness, Oonalaska; but, who is happy here below? However, I cannot complain against my fortune, when I think that all the powers of the world cannot affect your kindness towards me. Yes, Oonalaska, it is forbidden for us to see each other once more; it would do nothing but increase our passion; but, I carry into my solitude, the consoling idea that you will never forget me. It is neither distance, nor length of time, which can disunite our souls. Time, whilst it wrinkles our faces, purifies our thoughts; and, in strengthening our reason, will endear more and more our friendship. But, although I think with Chateaubriand: "L'âme a besoin, pour se développer dans toute sa force, d'être ensevelie quelque temps sous les rigueurs de l'adversité;" nevertheless, the pain of our separation is beyond my philosophy.... What more? I cannot even have the pleasure of explaining the cause of my absence in compliance with your request.

LORENZO.

TO LORENZO.

Coligny.

At last my father has told me the cause of your absence! Lorenzo, a father has a thousand claims on his children; but, he cannot have that of separating the soul of his child from that which nature has created for her happiness. Politic has nothing to do with us, Lorenzo. Views, either of integrity, ambition, wealth, or whatsoever interested ones which bring men to follow different kinds of governments, must have no influence with the force of our sympathy. Our souls cannot subsist, unless united.

On the other side, I cannot blame you, Lorenzo, since the oath which you took before your father is sacred, and, I do not think I would be happy with you, if for the sake of our love you would perjure yourself. My father has no such ties. And, why should he not be our friend, though differing in political sentiments?... But, as I know my father's character, I do not believe he would renounce his opinions even for my sake, who, after my mother, am the object of his most kind affections.

Lorenzo, why shall we not be happy? My father, my mother are the most sacred and dearest persons to me: but for you, Lorenzo, I feel something which, for want of a heavenly language, I cannot explain…. No, I shall never be able to live without you: "ou je m' attache, ou je me meurs." … If you have no objection, I am ready to follow you in any comer of the world you think proper.

OONALASKA.

TO OONALASKA.

Geneva.

Hélas, cette tende mère habite de l'autre côté de ces flots; peut-être qu'en ce moment elle les contemple du rivage opposé, en songeant à son fils!   *Chateaubriand.*

I feel as you the power of your reason, Oonalaska, when parents prevent so sacred tie, with no other reason but their caprice, I find no blemish in the side of two objects like ourselves when they follow their propensity. But, Oonalaska, in spite of it I would not be happy, under the idea of being a betrayer, by having abused the confidence of your father, who, knowing my principles, sleeps quiet in his bed without the least idea that I would run away with his dear daughter. You too, Oonalaska, would not be happy with me when far from your desolate parents. We are often bad judges of our own feelings before success; but when it is accomplished, we always feel a remorse in our conscience. Oonalaska, your love would not permit you to reproach me in not having prevented such a step; but, I should have the complaint of seeing you fainting every day: your feeling would kill you. On another side, I should pay with ingratitude the friendship and hospitality of your kind father. No, Oonalaska, we could not be happy. Angel of my painful existence, I would prefer not only a thousand deaths, but even to be forgotten by you, rather than bring the sorrow and the desolation into the bosom of your parents.

LORENZO.

Quelquefois je me persuade que l'Être-Suprême a abandonné le monde aux méchans, et qu'il a réservé l'immortalité de l'ame seulement pour les justes.   *Destaël.*

Among the sceneries which I would always like to see, it is one about a mile from Geneva on an elevated ground near the conflux of the Rhone with the Havre. Whilst I sat down on a small piece of green over a ravine cut down perpendicularly to the brink of the Rhone, sometimes admiring the line of demarcation going down for a long tract between the two distinct colours of the rivers, and sometimes observing on my left water of the lake flowing into the Rhone between Coutance, and Place Bel-air, I was surprised on discovering behind me an old friend of mine, Camillo, an Italian emigrant, father of a large family. He sat with me, and told that once Lorenzo was on the very piece of ground uttering the following monologue:

"I am unhappy, very unhappy! The companion of my thoughts is taken from me for ever. Oonalaska did never misunderstand me... But, why shall I wait a malady to put an end to this insupportable life? Why shall I live when the sacrifice of my country is consumed?"

After a long pause, said Camillo, he sat down on the green, and taking a Bible from his pocket, he read with great attention: then he thought for a long while, and read again smiling bitterly: at last he uttered:

"No, thou art not the God the heart of my dear mother has described to me, when, without experience, and insensible of the happiness which surrounded me, I knew nothing but the pleasure of a lively existence. No, thou art not that just, and good Creator that the goodness of my sister was pleased to pen with the colours of her angelical soul. A stoic would be ashamed of thy wrath. Yes, I have a better idea of God: but, since I cannot admire him as a being separated from matter, and invisible to me, my God is every good thing coming from his mysterious hand. When I shall see him not like a passionate man condemning the poor to be stoned in the wilderness because he gathered a few sticks on Saturday, but, with more justice, to exterminate with his thunderbolts the vile tyrants of my country, then I will believe in Moses. But, how shall I worship him, who with an eye of indifference assists such wretches on thrones, who soak themselves in human blood?"

Saying this, he flung the Bible into the river. But, when I saw him on the brink of a precipice, in the act of throwing himself, I cried:

"Senseless Lorenzo, such was not the counsel I gave you, when you came in my poor hut to give me the bread which delivered me from death. Your tears infusing in my heart a balm which gave life to my decaying days, made me feel the power of virtue, and I blessed heaven. Without the school of misfortune, I would have never been able to feel the celestial propensity of your fine soul. Oh, in another moment, Lorenzo, you would be ashamed of the idea of killing yourself. Although society is ungrateful to you, still you ought to be generous towards her by sparing your precious life. Look at me: I am more unhappy than you: old, exiled like you; but, you have no wife, no children as I have, without hope of doing my duty towards them: nevertheless, oftener I bless the hand which prolongs this miserable life."

He closed his eyes, and fell senseless into my arms. I

leaned him on the green; and seeing he was receiving new strength, I put his head on my knees, and he fell asleep. Sometimes I saw very violent emotions passing through his mind, and then I was willing to awake him: but, seeing that from time to time he was taking a periodical rest, I waited until he returned from his lethargy, I went with him to his house; and, in entering his closet, I had the satisfaction to see that his face was getting cheerful in reading with me the Divine Comedy of Dante. However, knowing his heart, I could not avoid thinking, whilst the unhappy young man was pleased in seeing virtue residing among those conspicuous men, whose life was nothing but a long string of vicissitudes, he was drinking the bitter chalice of his despair. Virtuous men had always suffered among their generations inferior to them of three or four centuries, by being their ignorant age in contradiction with them: besides, vice dislikes those, who would bridle it.

TO CHARLES.

Geneva.

Socrate, condamné par un jugement inique à perdre la vie dans quelques heures, n'avait pas besoin d'examiner bien attentivement s'il lui était permis d'en disposer. En supposant qu'il ait tenu réellement les discours que Platon lui fait tenir, croyez moi, Mylord, il les eût médités avec plus de soin dans l'occasion de les mettre en pratique, et la preuve qu'on ne peut tirer de cet immortel ouvrage aucune bonne objection contre le droit de disposer de sa propre vie, c'est qua Caton le lut par deux fois tout entier la nuit même qu'il quitta la terre.

J. J. Rousseau.

Yes, Charles, we must be out of our sense for such an unnatural act. A few weeks ago, had not Camillo run to my assistance, I would have committed suicide! and then what black stain I would have left beyond my grave! Now, I may say with Young:

> How poor, how rich, how abject, how august,
> How complicate, how wonderful is man!

I was so overpowered with pains, that my reason has quitted my unsound mind!

Although the picture of heaven, which was presented me when a child, was quite inconsistent with my natural feeling, I allow that some religions give so fine poetical ideas of an eternal life, that finding so little comfortability on this globe, we take pleasure, without further demonstration, in sticking with our utmost energy to a better existence. Then, although we have never heard from thence, our imagination creates a thousand things inconsistent with our human nature, and, like the man building castles in the air, we confect every pleasing thing, according to our own fancy. The lustful Mahometans imagine Houris; the

warriors, fighting battles over the clouds; the few virtuous
men, a God rewarding human actions on a golden scale;
the fanatics, nobody rewarded but blind superstitious believers; the monastics, the distinctions of a royal court; so
that, whilst, according to our dissenting creeds, human nature must be changed, still, we imagine to satisfy hereafter
our earthly ruling passions, quite inconsistent with perfection. Habit has so great power upon us, that we have seen
prisoners, in the last day of their detention, begging for remaining their whole life. And to whom, although ungrateful, is not the country of his birth dear? How sweet is the
recollection of those places, the witnesses of our infancy,
where every thing smiled before us in those happy days.
Do you see that hill? There I walked one day with my father; he folded me in his arms, and I feel yet on my cheeks
one of his warm tears when he blessed me with a sigh, and
uttering with affection: "Please God to make this child
happy when fortune shall have separated him from my
embraces. Here, under this oak, my eldest sister gave me
the affectionate kiss of her innocence. But, where is now
my father?... My father? Behold; he sleeps the eternal slumber of the grave. Oh! why his bones are not buried in a free
country? Oh! that tomb binds me with love to Italy!   ...
Dear Italy, thou art overlaid with tyrants! And when will it
be granted me to shed tears on that stone, mixed with those
of Oonalaska? Oh, I would forget the pains, which by want
of her comfort, I did not endure with all that worthy, and
manly fortitude of my sex.... But, I cannot be a stoic; and if
so, I would open my bosom, and cast out such a useless
heart... With Oonalaska? Charles, she is taken from me for
ever! Shall I have the hope of her society in heaven? No,
Charles, we are too miserable, and selfish creatures for the
gift of immortality: go to church, and listen attentively to

him, whom they call the best preacher; and then, in the
very moment he preaches humility, thou wilt feel a disgusting sensation of his pride! Wouldst thou know the reason of it? It is, because instead of the love towards his wan-
dering sheep, he conceals in himself the wrath of Moses.

LORENZO.

TO LORENZO.

London.

Que ceux qui nous exhortent à faire ce qu'ils disent, et non
ce qu'ils font, disent une grande absurdité! Qui ne fait pas ce
qu'il dit, ne le dit jamais bien; car le langage du cœur qui touche,
et persuade, y manque.   *J. J. Rousseau.*

Yes, Lorenzo, I heard many clergymen, who excited
in me the very loathful sensations which you describe
in your last letter. As we find a great many, following pro-
fessions for which they have no vocation, so, we find
spouting orators of the church, who believe the true
source of rhetoric is nothing else but speaking loud, and
inveighing against writers, whom they could not, or
would not understand. Then, people instead of learning
good morals, and feelings worthy of a civilized nation,
they do nothing but to drink a poison which kills reason
in the bud. But, for the honor of a great many, professing
our faith, I believe they are good, and sincere followers of
Christ. However, it is useless to argue with you on this
subject, since, although your letter seems too severe, I
know that you think with me. What displeases me, is to
see you bereft of the hope to find your friends in heaven,
the expected remuneration of the virtuous.

If I were not acquainted with thee, I should never

believe a man could be virtuous with thy dreadful philosophy. I admire the sublimity of thy mind always connected with nature: but, believe me, my best friend, the day will come, in which I shall enjoy the sight of my dear Lorenzo crowned with heavenly flowers before God. Thy lovely sisters "Col sorriso del pago desìo,"[4] will set it on thy forehead. Thou art worthy, Lorenzo, thou, who dost good not only without the hope of other reward hereafter; but, shunnest even the pleasure of seeing thy virtuous actions remunerated with the approbation of those, whom thou esteemest. I have not thy virtue, Lorenzo; but, though without hope, perhaps, I should do nothing deserving, when I can reach the sublimity of thy philosophy, then it seems a good action cannot be meritorious if it is done with the slightest idea of recompense. On the other hand, it would seem, that God could not refuse an eye of complacency on those actions also, which we perform with purpose of reward, provided that we avoid the infernal propensity of the miser, or the Pharisee's pride; since the nature of man, a compound of good and evil, suspending him between heaven and hell, renders it almost impossible for him to divest himself entirely of all selfish considerations. However, if a good action dignifies a man when he does it for the love of true glory, it ranks him with angels, when he does it in secret with no other pleasure but to satisfy the liberal feeling of an education, and pure conscience like thine.

Thou art something superior to man; and if thou have a "patria," thou shouldst be ranked with Cato. Our age does not understand thee. When thou speakest, selfishness is so inveterate, that thy hearers become thy antagonists. Their actions being against society, and by consequence against themselves, they feel in thee nothing but a censor.

The soul which animates thy existence with heavenly

inspirations will be extinguished for ever? The more I ponder the Bible, the more I find the moral of Lorenzo, in being at variance with it, it cannot transgress the Maker of all. Thy Bible is Nature, thou sayest; therefore thou art on the Lord's side, because Nature is the first book emanated from the hands of God.

CHARLES.

TO HIS DAUGHTER AMALIA.

> Nessun maggior dolore
> Che ricordarsi de' tempi felici
> Nella miseria.
>
> *Dante.*

Thy sentiments have painted me the benevolent religion of thy mother, and I felt my heart throbbing as it did in the days of my first love, days which are gone, and will return no more! Tell me, my dear daughter; do my enemies insult her grave? Go thither, and cover it with the last flowers of autumn. I read thy letter, to Lorenzo; and when I arrived to the following passage which I take now the pleasure of transcribing, I had the consolation to see him better. "I would have been with you to deviate Lorenzo from the danger in which his misfortune was leading him; and lift up his noble heart to the greatness for which nature has created him, and make him feel that his soul is not fit for this earth, but, to fly into the immense space of God, of God, who called him from nothing to immortality!"

In the bosom of our family? We have no hope now of embracing you! Lorenzo thanks you for your kind feelings towards him; and tells you, whilst he acknowledges your moral, and true charity, he advises you to avoid the Jesuits disguised in a great many shapes.

This last night thou wert my tutelar angel, Amalia; it seemed I was with you all in the very garden, once our property: thou wert gathering flowers; and after having made a fine wreath camest to set it on my head with the comeliness of a grace of Albano. Without my dreams, I should be like a patient deprived of the intervals of calm. Do not be uneasy concerning me, my daughter: the pain does not endure always; and, when I am released, I feel all the happiness of a free conscience.

If you, who are now the only objects of my affections, were not separated from me, I would say with Bulwer:[5] "I am one to whom all places are alike; it matters not whether I visit a northern, or a Southern clime." But, your absence, my dear daughters, is too painful for my weak philosophy. The life of man is a very trifling thing! When boys, we aspire to manhood: and when this arrives, which comes but too soon, we suffer in seeing wrinkles on our forehead. Soon the hair becomes gray; and we find ourselves in uncomfortable old age daily awaiting, what? ... A tomb, which whilst, for me, it will put an end to my sufferings, still, in the very moment of my death, I shall bring with me the painful idea of leaving you behind in a state of indigence. Then, hope tells us: Thou shalt walk above the stars…. Let us drop the curtain for the time to come!

I received a letter from Hippolytus, the brother of Lorenzo. The poor children of Italy are now scattered around the globe, dying unnoticed! I will transcribe for you, only these few lines of him: "A pure air, and a smiling country were pouring in my heart a sweet melancholy, when we reached the top of a small mountain, our eyes were sometimes on the Indian sea, and sometimes on the gulf of Arabia. We went towards a hut, and saw in it an Italian emigrant lying nearly dead. A man, lifting up his head, and his beautiful daughter not yet twenty years of age, giving to the patient all those succours which that miserable abode could bestow: Before expiring he said, that in seeing Italians around him, he was dying not quite unhappy."

Be cheerful my daughters, in thinking that our friend Lorenzo has for me the same affection he had for his father: the benefits I receive from his hand are such, that whilst they give illustration of his gentility, interfere not with my delicacy.

CAMILLO.

> Poor child of danger, nursling of the storm,
> Sad are the woes that wreck thy manly form!
> Rocks, waves, and winds, the shattered bark delay;
> Thy heart is sad, thy home is far away.   *Campbell.*

The darkness of the night increased, as Lorenzo with his heart full of joy travelled towards the town of all his hopes. The moonlight began to enlighten his way, when he arrived within two or three miles of the lovely habitation of his mother, and sisters.

"Permit me, my God," said he, lifting his hands towards the starry sky, "to live till I have pressed my mother to my bosom!"

He arrived, running to the door where he had breathed for the first time the breath of existence... A melancholy silence was reigning in the house; and his sisters and little brothers were praying around his mother, who had expired a few hours before. The unexpected pleasure she received from the letter of her dear son, announcing his arrival, joined to the last painful period of her life, carried her to the grave. At that sorrowful sight, Lorenzo fell in the arms of his sisters, and brothers; and, folding Carlotta in his arms, he remained a long time without being able to utter a syllable.

After the burial, he climbed up the mountains. The cries of his grief sounded like the wolfs long howls; he was heard to utter the most piercing cries of a maniac. As in the following night a dreadful storm carried away

several large trees, and some enormous cliffs; some of the
former were found swimming along the Tiber;[6] and
some of the latter in the bottom of it, and a man shot
among the rocks, his sisters, and friends, after having
spent several months in making useless inquiries, and
been reported them he must have died, with the af-
flicted situation of being deprived of the sad satisfaction
of burying so dear a brother, erected to his memory a
tombstone, which is now seen under two oaks, where he
used to sport in the happy days of his infancy. After five
or six months they received the following letter.

TO HIS SISTERS.

Lyons.

Si je regrette quelque chose dans la vie, ce sera de ne plus
aller sur le mont Ithome voir les troupeaux avec mon père, de
ne pouvoir nourrir l'auteur de mes jours dans sa vieillesse,
comme il me nourrit dans mon enfance.   *Chateaubriand.*

Our persecutors did not permit me to mourn with
you our dear mother. When we were in the church-yard,
one of our friends whispered in my ear, that two officers
were not far from us in search of me. I took immediately
the way of the Apennines: when I was not farther than ten
miles from you, I was assailed by the very officers: they
both discharged their arms on me; but, the souls of our
father, and mother must have shielded me, since I was
untouched: I killed one with my pistol, and put the other
to flight. I passed that stormy night on the Appennines,
protected by a rock. After five days, I reached Genoa; and,
with difficulty, went on board for Marseilles. I shall be
more diffused in my next letter.

LORENZO.

TO CHARLES.

Chatillon.

Ni les jours du printemps, ni l'azur des cieux, ni l'aspect des fleurs ne peuvent distraire l'âme d'une douleur profonde. Mais, le bruit du tonnerre plait au cœur déchiré par le désespoir; et lorsqu'au fort de nos peines un sanglot, un murmure s'échappent de nos lèvres, nous aimons à entendre la nature murmurer autour de nous, et le bruit des vents dans les cavernes, et des torrents sur la montagne couvrir la faiblesse de notre voix.

Le Barde.

Who called me on this globe to weep and die? My existence is nothing but a torture: I have here not a single person to whom I may pour out the bitter chalice of my sorrows which is undermining my life. I run upon this earth, like a hopeless extravagant; and every where find nothing but disgust: here, after my death, no friend will shed a tear on my eternal bed: time, says the philosopher, will heal the wounds death has given thee in cutting off thy best brother: he was kind to me, and when I bade him farewell, it was my last! My dear John!... My dear Carlotta too, is gone in heaven! This earth was too depraved for her; she could not survive our mother. Oh! how dreadful is the idea, that I shall see them no more! I shall not hearken to the sweet sound of their melodious voices, which often poured in my heart the balm of life.

The wind, and lightning raged sometime ago on the hill; a river from heaven has overflowed the dale: cattle, and men were drowned, or suffocated, whilst I was gazing on the destruction with apathy.

LORENZO.

TO AMALIA.

Geneva.

It is not without interest to observe in those remote times, and under a social system so widely different from modem—the same small causes that ruffle, and interrupt the course of life, which operate so commonly at this day; the same inventive jealousy, the same cunning slander, the same crafty and fabricating retailings of petty gossips, which so often now suffice to break the ties of the truest love, and counteract the tenor of circumstances most apparently propitious. When the bark sails on over the smoothest wave, the fable tells us of the diminutive fish, that can cling to the keel, and arrest its progress; so it is ever with the greatest passions of mankind: and we should paint life but ill, if, even in times the most prodigal of romance, and of the romance of which we must largely avail ourselves, we do not also delineate the mechanism of those trivial, and household springs of mischief, which we see every day at work in our chambers, at our hearths. It is in these, the lesser intrigues of life, that we mostly find ourselves at home with the past.   *Bulwer.*

The above citation is sadly true, my dear Amalia. They are but spoiled children of nature, whose life has always been a cheerful day of spring. Oh! this world is wicked, my dear! Now, that Lorenzo has left this place, a great many, who professed to be his friends, slander him with such an art, and cunning, that, if I were not thoroughly acquainted with him, they would even make me believe their lies.

A young man, careless of the insects around him, will easily lose his reputation, when a skilful foe, having the opportunity of entangling webs athwart his tracks, colours his innocent actions with infamy. There are many Iagos who feel an evil enjoyment, when they can see another Desdemona smothered by the hands of an Othello. Does an enemy tell a lie in a circle? Every one there present, whether he be of good faith, or wicked, in repeating, the same to others, will make it so public, that if the innocent were an Angel, he would not be able to wash out such a black stain. Since it is very easy to disrepute a stranger, I would punish every slanderer by the rigour of the law. It is related that a family, who understood the right of hospitality, learning that their present guest had murdered their father, after having given the wretch the means of quitting their roof, advised him not to meet them again, having determined to revenge the death of their father.

The evil that a bad tongue may cause to absent innocence, cannot be described, since human kind has a great propensity to listen to a slander with pleasure. It is a pity, Amalia, to see men, who would be silent before Lorenzo, now endeavoring to bring down his character. Every word, and every little action of him are distorted but to demolish his reputation. Nay: many have even the impudence to charge him with cowardice, as if we were not acquainted with the heroic deeds of Lorenzo. — The other day Mr X.... paid us a visit; and, speaking with my father, he said that Lorenzo had borne an insult without the least resentment. —Sir, I answered, it might be, that the virtue of Lorenzo, like Jesus, enabled him to endure an insult: but, I expected from you more delicacy towards him, since it has been told me, that it required Lorenzo's utmost efforts to the anger of Mr J...., who was determined to challenge you for an offence you had given him in a coffee-house.

I find, dear Amalia, my character is losing all the gentility of our sex in listening to so many detractors of a young man, whom I not only esteem, but, admire. If Lorenzo were not perfection itself, they would not take the trouble of slandering him. Indeed, Lorenzo once told me, that he would think highly of himself in proportion to the number of the enviers speaking badly of him. Amalia, it

seems, that when they find any man superior to themselves, they are not satisfied unless he be brought down
to their own common level. They would only speak
highly of him, if he were dead, or in a far country, where
he could not be their competitor in the circle of their society. And why so?... Because they are afraid, that every
lady, turning the back upon them, would admire their
virtuous antagonist. — Because, in a word, they understand these two lines of Shakespeare:

> "He hath a daily beauty in his life,
> That makes me ugly."

We have in history the most striking example of such
wickedness. When Aristides was condemned to ostra-
cism, a man not being able to write, called the very Aristides to put his name on the shell. "Do you know him,"
said Aristides to the unlettered? "No," was his answer.
"Why, then, will you banish him." "Because," said the
idiot, "I am tired of hearing people calling him the Just."

But, what would you say, if I tell you, that the hypo-
crite whom you know, has done all in his power to injure
Lorenzo's character in the sight of my father? However,
since they judge us so mean by listening to the detraction
of those, who delight in slandering the absent, I willingly
answered with irony, that I wanted a husband for this
world, and that I cared not, should he go to hell in the
next, provided he leave me to enjoy the paradise of his
honesty, and integrity on earth.

Few days ago, I went to Mrs A.... Before this my last
visit, I believed she had a fine education; but, her last conversation obliges me to think, that all her wealth will
never constitute her a lady. Some body present, speaking

disparagingly of Lorenzo, she said, that once, hearing, as she supposed under the vestibule the voice of Mr R...., she rose from her chair to meet him; but, when she saw it was but Mr Lorenzo C...., she could not avoid laughing at her mistake; and, having been quite ashamed to have demonstrated too much politeness to the teacher of her boy, she told him to take a chair under the vestibule. However, she said, I was very much pleased in seeing, that he, my politeness not going farther, in putting on his hat, and looking at me with a smile of contempt, went away without uttering a word. So that, she proceeded, I had the pleasure of getting rid of him. My heart was too deeply wounded, Amalia, in that moment, to find words adapted to such an occasion: I rose, and begged my mother instantly to leave the house.

I learned after two or three days, that the faults of Lorenzo was, not having reciprocated the love she had for him, and taught Greek, and Latin to her boy for nothing. I would hint to every body willing to speak badly of him, that since they are not angels, they have no reason to speak uncharitably even of those, who have really the very faults they are tickling to produce in public.

Come to England with me: your father Camillo would not hesitate, if you, and your sisters were determined.

OONALASKA.

TO CHARLES.

Chatillon.

But, what heart can conceive, what tongue utter the sequel? Who is that yonder, buffeted, mocked, and spurned? Whom

do they drag like a felon. Whither do they carry my Lord, my
King, my Saviour, and my God? And will he die to expiate those
very injuries? See where they have nailed the Lord, and giver of
life? How his wounds blacken, his body writhes, and heart
heaves with pity, and with agony! Oh Almighty sufferer, look
down, look down from thy triumphant infamy! Lo, he inclines
his head to his sacred bosom! Hark, he groans! See, he expires!
The earth trembles, the temple rends, the rocks burst, the dead
arise. Which are the quick? Which are the dead? Sure nature,
all nature is departing with her Creator.   *Steele.*

From the earliest period of history, we find learning
and theology intimately connected. The Bible was the
only instruction among the Jews, as well as the Iliad, and
Koran among Heathens, and believers in Mahomet.
With the progress of ages, sciences, and arts, taking a
more extensive ground, and giving a more exact idea of
natural things, in many parts inconsistent with the
above books, and more suitable to the refined ideas of a
more, and more educated people, created another class
of men of letters, who, assuming the name of philosophers, and grounding their reason on natural knowledge,
could not, and I think will never agree with the former,
who, not minding the real work of God, which is in the
nature itself, stand like champions to defend either the
Bible, Iliad, Koran, Ossian, Zemi, and the long sequel of
creeds without number. These theologers by a punctilio
which always springs either from ignorance, pride, or interest, whilst they close the ears to any other reason than
their own, in wishing, with the arm of terror to stop the
progresses of human mind, became so great enemies of
well grounded instruction, that we have only to open
history, if we want a disgusting view of morals mixed
with the most tyrannical actions a bloody-minded man

can produce. Thence two classes of men of letters in contradiction with each other: So, Reason, the only Divinity
we received from above to soothe our miseries, by being
presented in so many shapes, inconsistent with the laws
of the common mother Nature, does nothing but aug-
ment our woes. Thence every thing is inverted in the
economy of human society: and whilst hypocrisy, and
superstition are turning the people towards the life to
come, they endeavor to disregard the earthly present.
Certainly, I would say, we shall always have a subject of
complaint against the depravity of human society if we
have no regard to the improvements of our natural rights,
the very labor to which God put the human mind at work
with the example of the astronomical perfection. And,
would not, the justice of this earth, be a good preparation
for the life to come? — We cannot serve two Masters, they
say. — It is not so, I would answer: let reason improve society; and we shall see, that the very Lord of the earth is
the same one who formed the heaven: and since, according their own judgment, this earth is our first voyage to
celestial happiness, let us teach to the whole human race,
that we do not want tyrants to make us suffer here below
in order to sanctify with martyrdoms our religious virtues; but, having a more charitable feeling towards the
very ones, who, forgetting that heaven is open for them
too, cause the harmless virtuous man to suffer, by a
unanimous consent let us stand all on our rights with the
power of natural reason, with which God gifted us, and
force those poor, and wretched tyrants to become on the
way of a happy conscience: and plant flowers where our
idleness left growing thorns, and thistles.

Should we commit so many faults without the false notions of our own nature? The theoretical moral we are

taught in our education, being inconsistent with the theatre of human life, by want of this knowledge, of human heart, and of ourselves, we fall the victim of our ignorance.

The education I received from the embraces of my dear mother, forced me to commit a fault, Charles, which will bring me to another still grievous. Seeing from my childhood a predisposition of revenge, and resentment, she took great pains in inculcating me the heavenly moral of Jesus's forgiveness towards our persecutors: and, I became afterwards so enthusiastic of such a Christian virtue, that falling on my knees, I said with O. Goldsmith: "And now I see it was more than human benevolence, that first taught us to bless our enemies." How attractive was for me the heavenly benevolence of Christ! They laughed at, mocked, and spat on his face; and whilst he was dying on the cross, he asked pardon for the sins of his persecutors! It is grand, it is sublime, Charles; such goodness, it is the self-denial of a God! And whilst I write these lines, my tears drop on this paper for the love of Jesus! Even, supposed he was not the son of God; shall we not feel gratitude towards him, whose good intention, being for the improvement of society, his life had been the most striking example of morality?

As it was referred to you, it is true, I have been insulted: and, in that moment, the angelic soul of my dear mother being to my imagination with such an attractive influence, I did not repulse so gross an insult. Besides, the villain provoked me with such rascality of mean people, that whilst he wished to fight, he wanted to push me the first to challenge him for the right, as the law of duel prevails, of choosing the arms in which he is skilful. So, thinking with the following lines of Goldsmith too, I found the divine, and civil reason coincided together:

"You imagine, perhaps, that a contempt of your own life gives you a right to take that of another: but where, sir, is the difference between a duellist, who hazards a life of no value, and the murderer who acts with great security? Is it any diminution of the gamester's fraud when he alleges that he staked a counter?"[7]

All precepts might appear beautiful in theory; but, put it into practice, you will find it is not so. I learned afterward, when society does not provide for better, we ought not deviate from the laws of nature. As the Spectator is one of those rare books to whom civilization is very much indebted, I shall not produce it to you, as an object of my criticism: I would only say, that the declaration of his edict seems rather too particular against the challenger, whilst he inflicts no punishment to the aggressor. It seems to me, the rules of good society, and virtuous conversation are inverted not only from the very moment that an offended man writes a cartel; but, we must allow they have been inverted from the first slight, and trivial, as well as great, and urgent provocation. It is not the challenger I would put under the rigor of the law, provided he have a well grounded reason; it is the first provoker, unless asks pardon, or acknowledges his fault. As a brave man cannot be ungenerous, it is too painful for a polite society to see impertinents disregard a man of honour. Yes, Charles, since justice does not take an interested part by putting immediately her protecting hand without obliging one of the antagonists to the base act of denouncing his adversary, man is obliged to defend his own honour, unless he be the only support of a distressed family or occupying an eminent post useful to his country.

However, forgiveness of injuries will never be vile and shameful in the judgment of the few philanthropists:

but, should Rousseau have been stoned by the populace,
if they had thought to meet from himself, or from the law,
the due punishment of their rascality? Would we find so
much politeness, and respect if cowards were not checked
by the fear of meeting his man? Men would be like game-
cocks in a yard, without such a fear. But, let us listen to
Walter Scott on this subject.

"Wise men say, that we resign to civil society our natural rights of self-defence, only on condition that the ordi-
nances of law should protect us. Where the price cannot be
paid, the resignation takes no place. For instance, no one
supposes that I am not entitled to defend my purse, and
person against a highwayman, as much as if I were a wild
Indian, who owns neither law nor magistracy. The question of resistance, or submission, must be determined by
my means, and situation. But, if armed, and equal in force,
I submit to injustice, and violence from any man, high or
low, I presume it will hardly be attributed to religious, or
moral feeling in me, or in any one but a quaker. An aggres-
sion on my honour seems to be much the same. The insult,
however trifling in itself, is one of much deeper consequence to all views of life, than any wrong which can be
inflicted by a depredator on the high way, and redress is
much less in the power of public jurisprudence, or rather it
is entirely beyond reach. If any man chooses to rob Arthur
Mervyn of the contents of his purse, if he has not means of
defence, or the skill, and courage to use them, the assize at
Lancaster, or Carlisle will do him justice by taking up the
robber: yet, who will say I am bound to wait for this justice,
and submit to be plundered in the first instance, if I have
myself the means, and spirit to protect my own property?
But, if an affront is offered to me, submission to which is to
tarnish my character for ever with men of honour, and for

which the twelve judges of England, with the chancellor to boot, can afford me no redress, by what rule of law, or reason am I to be deterred from protecting what ought to be, and is so infinitely dearer to every man of honour than his whole fortune? Of the religious views of the matter I shall say nothing, until I find a reverend divine, who shall condemn self-defence in the article of life, and property. If its propriety in that case be generally admitted, I suppose little distinction can be drawn between defence of person and goods, and defence of reputation. That the latter is liable to be assailed by persons of a different rank in life, untainted perhaps in morals, and fair in character, cannot effect my regal right of self-defence. I may be sorry that circumstances have engaged me in personal strife with such an individual; but, I should feel the same sorrow for a generous enemy, who fell under my sword in a national quarrel. I shall leave the question with the casuists, however, only observing, that what I have written, will not avail the professed duellist, or he, who is the aggressor in a dispute of honour. I only presume to exculpate him, whom is dragged into the field by such an offence, as, submitted to in patience, would forfeit for ever his rank, and estimation in society."[8]

But, the philosopher, or to explain myself with a periphrasis adapted to my grateful feeling, the friend of my mind would reprove me by doing what my judgment disowns. And the following Fragment of my friend Manesca, will receive his approbation.

"What a fine thing courage is! I mean not that courage which braces up our energies, and enables us to work our way through civil life, amidst the difficulties which assail our moral career; that courage which cheers us in our industrious exertions, and too often unprofitable labours;

which assists us in our struggles against seduction, rescues us triumphantly from the clutches of vice, and guides us in the narrow path of virtue; — in short, that courage which sustains us with dignity in the various relations of husband, father, friend, and citizen. — No, I mean that brilliant, that dazzling courage, which prompts us to face and receive a bullet, or speed it through a man's heart, in order to demonstrate that we are men of honour. Honour! What is honour? Is it not the offspring of public respect? — Can Mr X.... be a man of honour, because he has been a principal in several duels? Has he not been twice a fraudulent bankrupt? Does he ever pay any debts except those which he contracts at the gaming table? Is any one ignorant that, by his irregular conduct, he has precipitated to his grave an aged parent; that he neglects his children, and his amiable wife, whose property he has squandered in nightly revels? All this is true; but Mr X... is at all times ready to pull a trigger; his courage is doubted by no one: he is an honourable gentleman. Then, after a long life of industry, and uprightness, notwithstanding that I have strictly fulfilled my duties as a dutiful son, a tender husband, a prudent and kind father, a sincere friend, and an honest citizen, I am unworthy of public respect; I am a dishonourable man, because I neither know how to fire a pistol, nor handle a sword; because I neither wish to kill nor be killed; because I tremble at the atrocious alternative of being a murderer, or of depriving my innocent family of their natural protector, and leaving them a prey to misery, and burthen upon society! O reason, reason, where art thou?

"This, indeed, is most unreasonable, it is absurd, but custom will have it so: we must submit. Custom! abolish it then. Is there any thing immutable but what is written in nature's laws? Ought not custom, anti-social ridiculous custom to disappear at the voice of reason and humanity?

"What is custom but a more or less general disposition regularly to act in certain circumstances? Custom,
therefore, is nothing but the result of opinion; but as the
latter, however general, may be erroneous, custom in an
enlightened community is amenable to the tribunal of
reason. — Opinion says, that gentlemen should never be
suspected of being deficient in courage. — Does opinion
say nothing else? Does she not say, that gentlemen should
never have quarrels? Does she not hold that excesses of
any kind are degrading, unbecoming well bred men?
Does she not bid a real gentleman refrain from hurting
the feelings of any one, and insist, that should be ever so
far to forget himself as to offer an insult, a manly apology
only can retrieve his character? In short, does not opinion
maintain that true magnanimity consists in pardoning
offences, and that genuine honour can be sullied by him
only, who possesses it, if he swerve from the line of conduct which has merited him public respect?

"Opinion needs no proof of the warlike courage of any
gentleman, for the plain reason that, except in those rare
circumstances, where national independence is threatened,
society has nothing to gain by the loss of one of its mem-
bers, social order should be the pole-star, of all opinions
whether private, or public; and warlike courage can be ra-
tionally fostered only in the case that it may be subservient
to social interest.

"A generous soldier, who exposes, and sacrifices his
life for his country, will ever be entitled to public respect;
but, it is yet to be proved that a duellist is necessarily a
valiant warrior: nay, many have been known to turn pale
before the common enemy, who confident in their skill in
taking aim, or handling a sword, were notorious duellists.

The famous St. George, in Paris, whom had been forbidden to fight duels, because he was sure to kill his antagonist, proved to be a coward at the head of a regiment of horse which he commanded.

"That sort of courage which prompts us to brave death is not natural; it is a feverish state to which all men are naturally adverse; but, to which they all may be stimulated by various artificial means, which respectively operate according to circumstances, and tempers. The vain gratification of winning the good opinion of some deluded contemporaries, is the stimulus which operates upon the duellist's brain; a mercenary soldier's courage may be lighted up with a little alcohol; nothing, in short, of the certainty of fulfilling a sacred duty to his country should stimulate a freeman.

"Can any one be so simple as to imagine, that the savage courage of braving death is the quality admired, and revered in great warriors? Many worthless fellows in the file, possess such a courage in a higher degree, than the superior, who leads them on. Patient industry, unconquerable perseverance through long, and laborious studies; a sacrifice of all worldly pleasures, in exchange for toils, cares, abstemiousness, anxieties, and sufferings; solid judgment, prudence, self-possession, great talents, still greater honesty; such are the offspring of the courage which recommends heroes to the veneration of ages.

"But, many superior men have fought duels.—So much the worse for them: their fair fame, most surely, is not indebted to such deeds. What then does the assertion prove? It proves only, that men of superior order are not free from weakness, and that, in all their actions, they are not worthy of imitation. If superior men, who fight duels are not aware that opinion, respecting that custom, is erroneous, they are deficient in good sense, and judgment, two qualities without which a man cannot be truly great: if, on the contrary, they know it to be wrong, they are doubly guilty in yielding to its mischievous caprice, when they should be the first to resist and correct it.

"A young man was heard to ask whether Napoleon was not a great master at the broad sword. Such are the silly notions which are too commonly entertained about great men. Napoleon never fought a duel. He dared in his youth, to set at defiance the brutish custom, and braved the scorn of his fellow officers; the pretenders to despise him — where are they?

"Washington, greater than Napoleon, — since his genius will, in the end, more generally obtain the veneration of mankind, — Washington never fought a duel; nay, it is well known, that he once made an unasked for apology to a person whose feelings, he thought, he had wounded. Franklin did not fight duels; yet Franklin was a gentleman, as well as a statesman, and philosopher. Perhaps he had never occasion to fight. Well, let genuine gentlemen in our days imitate him; let them prove their good breeding by scrupulously shunning all circumstances which might involve them in those despicable transactions; or, if unfortunately precipitated in those anti-social proceedings, let them adopt means of conciliation which may spare a family the loss of a father or husband, and society a useful citizen, which will insure them the gratitude, and respect of the sober portion of the community.

"But, it is not to be expected that the mere efforts of the individuals eventually concerned in these sad affairs, will be sufficient to put an end to the atrocious custom. Opinion which fosters it, should be resolutely assailed, and shamed out of the social pale. Novelists, poets,

dramatists, and writers in general, should join hand in
hand in this holy crusade. A great deal might be achieved
in this reform of public opinion, by those, who have the
charge of the education of youth, by the heads of families,
and particularly mothers.

"Women, O women! what could you not do? Like the
sun's rays upon nature, your influence in society is irre-
sistible; let it ever be vivifying, and cheering. O ye, who
give us life, never suffer death to emanate from you, and
by more than one attribute, resemble the beautiful luminary to which we dare to compare you."

It is with an edifying feeling I see in some corners of
the world the people listening with an anxious ear the
wishes of benevolent philosophers: and time, in spite of
legislators forgetful of their duty, bringing the nations to
more extensive instruction, will blot out the custom of duels as it has been done in regard to the vain glory of
knights fighting in the arena before the object of their
love. Nay: though it is with sorrow of mind we find, in
some countries, people going as spectators of such single
combats, others, where the public opinion is more enlightened, in spite of the law not pursuing such kind of
murders, still, shameful of such a ferocious act, they go
concealed fighting in the most remote woods. But, as we
are obliged to dress ourselves according to fashion if we
want not to appear ridiculous, so a man, whose fortune
depends from the respect of little minded plurality, is
forced to do what his reason disapproves. Besides, how
can a man, not only dependent, but exiled, abandoned,
unknown, poor, and friendless in a strange country scorn
the general custom? I shall never forget the poor unpro-
tected Jews of my still poorer country, whom the greater
part of Christians think it lawful to insult. Yes, Charles,

one day I could not refrain from rescuing a poor old Jew from the persecution of my school companions!

But, why shall I allege so many reasons, Charles, when my own example proves the evidence of my argument? After having endured so gross an affront, they had so scornful an idea of me, that every wicked creature did not lose the opportunity of showing his false bravery with petty insults. And what would you say, Charles, should I tell you, that villain, who insulted me, has been emboldened by hearing from others, that I had been much indulgent in forgiving the impoliteness of two others before him? Addison writing about the customs of his time, which were in many respects the same as ours, says: "The great point of honour in man is courage, and in woman chastity. If a man loses his honour in one encounter, it is not impossible for him to regain it in another; a slip in a woman's honour is irrecoverable." The moral Addison, conscious of the false notions of his age, added: I can give no reason for fixing the point of honour to these two qualities, unless it be, that each sex sets the greatest value on the qualification which renders them the most amiable in the eyes of the contrary sex. Had men chosen for themselves, without regard to the opinions of the fair sex, I should believe the choice would have fallen on wisdom, or virtue; or had women determined their own point of honour, it is probable that wit or good nature would have carried it against chastity." So, whilst I was displeased in seeing the severity of society towards women, whose fault might be caused either from disinterested love, want of judgment, or innocence, finding that the first opportunity would have carried me to recover my honour with so little an expense, that, in meeting in the street the first rascal, who thought to mock me with impunity, I pulled off my coat; and boxed him with such alacrity, that, though he was a bulky man, I had the satisfaction of see-ing him on the ground without, however, any mortal in-jury: So, the very mob, Charles, who would have scorned me if I had proceeded my way without resentment, after the fight, they were inclined to bring me in triumph.

But, what shall I conclude after so long a letter? Charles, when I was in the arms of my dear mother, I es-teemed men, and myself: the rascalities I met afterwards on the theatre of life, whilst they obliged me to pity myself, caused me to despise the whole human race: but, after a long reflection, finding human kind under improvements, though yet we are very far from deserving the honourable title of rational, or sociable creatures for which it seems we have been called on earth, still I begin to feel highly of man. But, until the mass of the people, in getting better judgment will have provided for better laws on the subject of duels, some individuals might be under obligations to stand be-fore death, rather to suffer an injury to their reputation.

LORENZO.

TO LORENZO.

Geneva.

Do ye imagine to reprove words, and the speeches of one that is desperate, which are as wind? *Job.*

Do not believe your soul mortal, Lorenzo: I do not pre-tend to defend one creed more than another; but, for what purpose could nature have given us a life so toilsome, and afterwards take it away for ever? O, this spirit which I feel within me, panting for immortality is fit to worship God:

he may have created in other planets, beings more sublime than man; but, the wish, and imagination able to understand the divine idea of the infinite, is enough to make us believe we are fit for an eternity. When I think of the greatness of this creation my mind would pass through the immense space of the ether, where the veil of my ignorance would be taken from my eyes, and contemplate the mysterious incantation.

OONALASKA.

A FRAGMENT FROM LORENZO.

Paris.

Any one may do a casual act of good nature, but a continuation of them shows it is a part of the temperature; and certainly, added I, if it is the same blood which descends to the extremes, touching her wrist, I am sure you must have one of the best pulses of any woman in the world.   *Sterne.*

She was knitting at the door of her shop: her smile reminded me of my candid sisters, whose acute sight was reading my heart's most secret thoughts. She rose from her chair; and with a kind-hearted look asked me if I wished to look at any thing. — I come to buy something, madam, which I have entirely forgotten. — You must have a great deal of business, sir, sit down. — She resumed her work, blushed, and remained silent for some time....

It seems by the above, and following letters, that many of it must have been lost.

TO LORENZO.

Lausanne.

J'ai les yeux sans cesse fixés sur les montagnes qui séparent la Suisse de la France; il vit par delà, mais il ne m'a point oubliée: la douceur de mes pensées me l'assure. Quand je me promène sous les voutes de la nuit, mes regrets ne sont point amers, et s'il avait cessé de m'aimer le frissonnement de la mort m'en aurait avertie.   *Mad. Destaël.*

Thou thoughtest of me! Every time I walked through these delightful fields, I did the same, and thy memory endeared my life. My heart embraced all nature, and nature smiled on me. How many times I sent my heart to thee on the wings of my thought, and then I felt the ambrosia exhaling from the plants, and a zephyr caressing my forehead. If our souls were not immortal would I have felt such sympathy? When on the mountains of Swizerland thou feltest an inebriate pleasure of divinity, it was thy soul, which flying to me made me feel the joy thou wishedest impart to me.

OONALASKA.

TO OONALASKA.

Ingouville.

Tu m'appeleras toujours quand tu seras seule. Plusieurs fois tu répéteras le nom de Léonce, et Léonce recueillera peut-être dans les airs les accens de son amie.   *Destaël.*

That which most deeply wounds my feeling, is to see moral perverted by the hand of men, who, under the cloak of piety, slander those, whom they believe in contradiction with their hypocrisy. However, I think with Destaël: "Je dédaigne ceux qui me blâmeront; ils ne m'atteindront pas dans l'asile de mon cœur où je suis content de moi; ils n'ébranleront point cette parfaite conviction de l'esprit qui est aussi une conscience pour l'homme éclairé."[9] I have some moments, Oonalaska, in which, by want of your company, who would partake my sentiments, the above conviction not only is not sufficient; but, instead of pouring the balm of life into the wound with which false piety has deeply poisoned the vital centre of my heart, it does oftener exacerbate it, in thinking my self-denial led me a victim of monsters in human shapes.

Every thing in your possession must turn in your favour, because a society dreaming nothing but wealth, forgive even your virtue, which is a reproach for them. But, I poor, without other merit in the world but the good intention of practising virtue, I would bring into your private family but the envy of the wicked without number. "The world is made for Cæsar," exclaimed the virtuous Cato, few moments before his glorious death: in our age we may say, the world is made for wealthy people.

When troublesome thoughts will agitate thee, look upon the star which precedes the day break: often I do the same, and then I feel relieved.

It is a religion for every body: it does not reside in books; it speaks in our hearts, and tells us this sufficient precept: Love thy fellow creature. Because our ancestors began human society with superstitions, some of our legislators believe it cannot be otherwise; and consider every body wicked, because in spite of Solon, Lycurgus, Brutus, Cato, Machiavel, Bentham, we are still not better than the time of Moses. But, I would ask only one single question: Has the people been ruled by the laws of the above legislators, or by that of Moses? Nay; because our forefather's government was a perfect theocracy they are led to conclude that the foundations of human laws should be grounded on those principles, and think it cannot be otherwise since it had always been so. Then, they call the man a wicked creature, without thinking that all human faults originate in a neglected education. They are like that father, who, whilst obliges his sons to perish by hunger, upbraids them because they cannot stand up.

Man is but the creature of his habits: and, we find slaves, after having received liberty, to submit themselves again to their own masters. When will man enjoy the confederacy of man? — Then, our posterity in reading history will conceive all the horrors of our situation. If I have the happiness of seeing the dawn of so fortunate a day, I would not complain on my death bed of the ingratitude of my fellow Beings: I would carry to my grave the idea, that I shall not be entirely forgotten.

It is no wonder if we are continually in war; since, spoiled from contrarieties without number, we must feel our wicked selfishness from the bosom of our mothers. Thence, sensibility becomes a fatal gift when we are forced to live with people with a little heart; love, which endears life, becomes an object of calculation, and friendship a hypocritical name.

The original sin, Oonalaska, is the want of education. Reason is a star which leads us to virtue: and although she cannot reach her destination soon as we would, she always leaves on her way the brilliant traces of her painful, and noble career: nothing deserving reproach on the grave of her sons.

Havre is built on a marsh; and the harbour being surrounded of a rampart, I am obliged to climb the hill of Ingouville whenever I wish to contemplate the beauties of nature. What fine month of November!

I prove a very singular sensation every time I present myself in a hotel in which hospitality is given with more, or less kindness according to the extensiveness of your purse. They measure all travellers from foot to cap; and elevate them towards heaven, according to the exterior appearances of their travelling expenses. Such is their acuteness, that they are seldom found putting a Lord on the seventh, or a Burgess on the first floor; so that, from the first floor to the garret, where all pedestrians are confounded, you would know the standing of each traveller in society by the several degrees of their rooms: and the landlord is more or less cheerful with you, according to the quantity of money you spend. If in the New-world I shall not find better people, I will go on the top of a mountain to breathe the air embalmed with flowers.

Yesterday evening I clambered up the bill to the light houses: I set near a ravine where the sea touches the foot. A light north wind was driving a great many ships on the lee shore of France. Crows, and eagles were hovering, when I saw a pigeon preceding a vessel: perhaps that bird was bringing news to some more happy than I in France.... More happy than I? ... Although alone, thy image is always with me.

The sinking sun told me I must leave that place: I had yet two hours of walk to reach Havre, and no more than an hour of day. As I wanted to see the sun sinking in the flood, in going back I took another road. I gave him the good night, and reached the hotel at dinner time.

After my solitary reflections on the top of a hill, I do not like to see at the table, fops fond of distinguishing themselves by causing the servants to feel their inferiority before them. It seems they sit at the table of four francs, not to satisfy their want; but, to play the gentlemen.

To-day a captain of a vessel, father of a large family, having some difficulties with a man of the vexing custom-house, brought the quarrel to a duel: he was killed instantly. The officer of the custom-house is not persecuted by the law.

There is a pleasure in sorrow: it is the shivering mixt with tears in the very moment we are quitting, perhaps for ever, persons worthy our friendship: the last day of a man with pure conscience, must be the moment of his happiness.

Farewell, Oonalaska: do not be afraid for me: the passage I undertake now, is very well known. How sublime is the ocean! When the shore of France will have disappeared from my sight, still, I will give thee the good-bye.

I cannot proceed longer; the vessel is now ready to start.

LORENZO.

It seems here some other letters must have been lost.

————————————————

TO CHARLES.

Philadelphia.

Or qual estranea mai lontana terra,
E selvaggia, ed inospita pur sia,
Increscer puote a chi la propria vede
Schiava di crude, ed assolute voglie?

Alfieri.

I cannot describe the painful feeling occasioned by being far from the remains of my distressed family. It is not the tyrants of my country I left under that blue sky; it is the dear house of my father. I may say now with Petrarch:

"Exul ab Italia furiis civilibus actus
Hue subii, partimque volens, partimque coactus.
Hie nemus, hie amnes, hie otia ruris amœni:
Sed, fidi comites absunt vultusque sereni."

Nobody will impart to me the affection I enjoyed from my father, mother, brothers, and sisters. The whole world seems to me a desert now: where shall I find a friend to whom I might communicate my sufferings?... However, I walk this wide world thinking with Casimir Bonjour:

"Je sais qu'il est beaucoup d'âmes intéressées,
Que l'argent est au fond de toutes les pensées;
Mais, j'ose l'assurer, il est de nobles cœurs."[10]

In answer to your letter, dear Charles, certainly no nation deserves theconsideration of a civilized one, if she, in spite of discordant superstition, does not honour, and help the true, moral, unsuperstitious, sincere, and innocent man. — Cowper says:

"The only amaranthine flower on earth
Is virtue; the only lasting treasure, truth."

LORENZO.

———————————————————

TO OONALASKA.

Philadelphia.

As the persecuted seek refuge at the shrine, so they recognised in the altar of their love an asylum from the sorrows of earth.   *Bulwer.*

By the interference of Charles, I received your letter.
If there is any disgusting sensation, it is the recollection of
those who were ungrateful to us. I had formed an idea
too sublime of man; but, how humiliating is the selfishness of human species!

"Ubique pavor, et plurima mortis imago,"

Says Virgil. However, I thank the heavenly Hope for
having led me by the hand through this life of dangers;
and told me I shall find the virtue I am seeking for.

I found myself alone on a barren rock surrounded by
a sea without end; and the fainting light of virtue, agreeable delusion of my passed life, was now too far away.
Every day I felt my chains more and more heavy. When a
supernatural strength overwhelms us, courage fails.
What avails to struggle for life, when the wound is mortal? Why, my God, said I, didst thou create me but for sufferings? Hast thou made the world only for my oppressors? O! your letter, Oonalaska, has changed my sufferings of hell into the enjoyments of Eden!

Poor Malvina! Yesterday she was shining like the sun;
and now, under ground!. All this smiling family of plants
which surrounds her grave, does not now cheer her sensibility; and tears can warm her bosom no more!

Excuse me, my love, if I do not write to thee on the
manners and customs of this nation: excuse me, if I do not
describe to thee these fine mountains: every thing is sublime because I am thinking of thee. Yes, this beautiful
nature should be a desert without the thought of thy love:
every time I am occupied in something, I see only thy
inspiring image: and how could I be able to write were
it not about thy amiability. Very often, absorbed in the

fine ideal which surrounds thee, my pen falls, believing thou art in my presence.

P. S. The sun was sinking when the groom came to tell me, my horse was ready. I had forgotten, that I gave him order to do so…. However the moon is up, and I have no more than about 15 miles to reach my society in the country.

Every evening I contemplate the planet which shines in the twilight: when at ten o'clock it leaves our horizon, I feel the sensations I had when I bade thee farewell: it is as pretty as thy thought. Dear Oonalaska, look at it also, when quivering it bids thee good night. It appears to me I am still with thee walking around by the lake of Geneva with thy arm linked in mine, gazing at the silent moon…. Well, the groom tells me the vessel will not start from America to France in a week; so that, I will not yet seal this letter.

P. S. Yesterday, seeing all society smiling at my distractions, however they are kind to me, and at that moment hearing to strike ten o'clock, I hurried out, without taking leave, with the intention of going back, after having gazed on the lovely planet. The harmony of the sky bringing to my mind so delightful an idea of thee, I proceeded homeward without my hat, fearing the presence of any body else should have interrupted the lovely sentiment I proved in that moment: the dream I had of thee the last night was heavenly as thy smile, I shall attempt in another letter to describe it.

P. S. To-night the planet, which calls me to happiness, disappeared above the clouds, leaving me in darkness, and bitterness.

LORENZO.

TO HIS BROTHER HIPPOLITUS.

Philadelphia.

Quand on veut consacrer des livres au vrai bien de la patrie, il ne faut point les composer dans son sein.

J. J. Rousseau.

Do not yet attempt to emulate the splendid style of
any author, who has dazzled you: your tender age is not
fit to follow the eagle in his flight. No strong passion if
you do not feel it: write according to your own heart.
Your age is only fit for an ingenious sensibility, which is
always agreeable when you exhibit it in its natural sim-
plicity: no exclamations; no tropes, no figures: write as if
you were explaining your feeling with the sincerity of a
soul before the Great Judge of human secrets; and your
writing will be eloquent.

If you wish to run the difficult career of learning,
form your heart, and nothing will be wanting: but, if we
do not feel in ourselves nobility, and sublimity of mind,
the attempt will be always a disgraceful one: it is the fire
of heaven alone, which can purify the mind of man. Europe, my dear brother, swarms now too much with pre-
tensions to learning: but, if the writer's aim is not that of
being useful to society, this noble art is nothing but a pro-
fane prattle.

When you have finished the course of your studies, if you don't feel yourself able to soar towards the
sun, you may turn your thoughts elsewhere. In whatever
situation a man finds himself, either of mind, or fortune,
he may be always happy, if he do not swerve from the
knowledge of himself, right, and honesty. As we can always distinguish the beginning of the day, even in the

most cloudy weather, so, in spite of wicked enemies, virtue will always have the consideration, and esteem of every nation. It is not an elevated occupation, which gives consideration to man; it is the little, performed with integrity: and, should there be no suitable judges for your actions, comfort yourself in your superiority, and always endeavor to become better. "Knowledge will always predominate over ignorance, as man governs the other animals," says Johnson.

Do not bewail our situation, dear Hippolitus: man is born to undergo inconveniences: misfortune is a great school for those, who are wise to learn from it: a life spent among books in all the comforts of the closet, may fit a man for becoming an astronomer, or artist; but, he will be always ignorant of himself, and of the human heart. It is true, that when we reach the knowledge of it, we would desire to retrograde to the sports of our infancy, in which we believed all men had towards us the very affection of our father, and mother: but, who would desire this happy ignorance when we find ourselves daily obliged to have something to do with them?

If you feel in yourself the demon of genius, you will have nothing in your life but cares, and disgusts. The way to glory is easy among people, who enjoy a real liberty: but, if you speak truth where despotism reigns, you have nothing to expect but ingratitude. Who would believe, Hippolitus, that Volney, that great luminary of human reason is yet slandered after his grave? And, did he write any thing but to teach us the means of being happy, and honest on earth? These few lines are sufficient to show his integrity. "Recherchez des lois que la nature a posées en nous pour nous diriger, et dressez-en l'authentique, et immuable code; mais, que ce ne soit plus pour une seule nation, pour une seule famille; que ce soit pour nous tons sans exception! Soyez le législateur de tout le genre humain, ainsi que vous seriez l'interprète de la même nature, montrez-nous la ligne qui sépare le monde des chimères de celui des réalités, et enseignez-nous, après tant de religions, d'illusions, et d'erreurs, la religion de l'évidence, et de la vérité."[11] But, it is not only our misunderstood creed, which perse-cutes the benevolent philosophy; so Pananti:[12] "Maometto è il più gran nemico che la religione umana abbia avuto. Uomini pieni del suo feroce spirito esclamarono che Dio punirebbe il Califfo al Mamon per avere appellato nei suoi stati le scienze a detrimento della santa ignoranza raccomandata ai veri credenti: e che, se qualcuno osasse imitarlo, impalar si doveva, e di Tribù in Tribù trasportarlo, preceduto da un Araldo, che andasse ad alta voce gridando: Ecco quale è stato, e quale sarà il guiderdone dell'empio, che preferisce la Filosofia alla Tradizione, e la sua superba Ragione ai precetti del divino Koran." However the martyrs of Reason will prevail on the martyrs of superstition. So Franklin: "It is only by degrees that the great body of mankind can be led into new practises, however salutary their tendency. It is now nearly eighty years, since inoculation was introduced into Europe and America, and it is so far from being general at present, that it will, perhaps, require one, or two centuries to render it so."

The glory of fame is a very trifling thing, since there are few, who in reality admire the worthy work of a great man; So Bulwer: "Often, when in the fever of the midnight, I have paused from my unshared, and unsoftened studies, to listen to the deadly pulsation of my heart, when I have felt in its painful, and tumultuous beating the very life warning, and wasting within me, I have sickened to my inmost soul to remember, that amongst all those, whom I was exhausting the health, and enjoyment of youth to benefit, there was not one from whom my life had an interest, or by whom my death would be honoured by a tear." Again, a genius like that of Homer will have very little consideration, when his book is among a thousand others equal to it. There is no human strength which can scorn the power of time.

But, if in spite of your happiness you wish to show to the people among whom you live, that they are far from deserving the approbation of a worthy society, you ought to recollect, that the boys of an academy have very little friendship towards their teacher for no other reason than that, he is in the habit of correcting their faults. What are men among vicious laws?—Large boys hardened in their vices. They will grant you every justice, or injustice against others; but, if you do not vilely flatter their own faults, and self-interest, they will become your enemies. See, even among republics, the many are attached to the richest party, because they fear to lose their direct interest with the wealthy people. Ignorance is deceived by want of knowing a gentleman among cunning rascals: and you would hear in America, men calling those Yankees, whom they dislike, whilst they are Yankees themselves in all the extensiveness of the term. As I suppose you are not acquainted with this word, I will endeavour to explain it to you.

Hearing in this country to utter the word Yankee with contempt, I referred to the American dictionary, in which it is said, the Indians, or originated savages of America, in consequence of being unable to pronounce the word English, they said Yankee. Afterwards it became a word of contempt applied by settled European-Americans to every stranger from Europe: so, by a spirit of revenge, an English

author calls Yankees the Americans smoking Havana's to-
bacco on sugar bales. But, not satisfied of this explanation,
by seeing so many, giving different colours to this word, I
asked several persons; and, the most inoffensive idea under such word, I found it was the supposed Americans
from north in respect to those from south. For instance, the
New-Englanders would be Yankees to the New-Yorkers,
the New-Yorkers to the Pennsylvanians; these to the Virginians, the Virginians to the Carolinians, and so on. If it
were so, though the offence trifling in itself, I would prefer
to be under the equator's line where those, who are in this
side of North America have no right to call me a Yankee, a
word which, even pronounced by persons of the most high
education, does not sound to my ear a kind one. In regard
to those, who call Yankees the strangers coming into America, they must offend themselves, since the American blood
is stranger to this country. You know, Hippolitus, Switzerland not being able to afford enough for all her inhabitants,
they are obliged to live in France, and Italy with their industry. In America such kind of people would be baptized
Yankees. Among persons of education they call only Yankees now, those cunning creatures, who are getting money
with deceit: and it seems to me, in this last case, such degrading title, is very happily applied. The foundation of
America being a wise liberty, and a compact of true United
States, all the petty lines of demarcation disappear with
general instruction; and every true American feels pleasure
in seeing every nation having a reciprocal consideration of
each other. This little globe turning around, the very inconsistent Being called Man improving, must feel the noble
sentiment of becoming a true citizen of the world: so, now
a Yankee is generally called a poor creature, who is far
from understanding the feeling of a gentleman.

But, for what reason a philanthropist is paid with ingratitude, whilst the selfish becomes rich? Oliver Goldsmith will show you in the following lines, that sometimes
flattery has power even over wise men: "Upon returning
home, I could not help reflecting with some astonishment,
how this very man, with such a confined education, and
capacity, was yet capable of turning me as he thought
proper, and moulding me to his inclinations! I knew he
was only answering his own purposes, even while he attempted to appear solicitous about mine; yet, by a volun-
tary infatuation, a sort of passion compounded of vanity
and good nature, I walked into the snare with my eyes
open, and put myself to future pain, in order to give him
immediate pleasure. The wisdom of the ignorant, somewhat resembles the instinct of animals; it is diffused in but
a very narrow sphere, but within that circle, it acts with
vigour, uniformity, and success."

If you take the hard career of being a deserving writer,
after your death, you might receive the honour of a stone
on which the virtuous like yourself, among posterity will
shed a tear for reconciling your insensible bones to mankind; and perhaps a poet might sing your virtues; the only
wreath reserved to the children of true glory: still, although
"Non vive oltre la tomba ira nemica," as Monti says if your
generous feeling excites you to demonstrate the evil that
society undergoes under the scourge of an ignorant, and
false religion, after your death you may expect to be slandered by those, who find their interest in telling the people,
that Hume, Volney, Rousseau, and other illustrious writers, are now burning in hell. And, for what reason have we
the displeasure of hearing from the pulpit such kind of language, if it is not by having those superior men written the
truth, as these few lines of the historian Hume! "Monastic

observances were esteemed more meritorious than the active virtues: the knowledge of natural causes was neglected, from the universal belief of miraculous interpositions, and judgments: bounty to the church atoned for every violence against society: and the remorses for cruelty, murder, treachery, assassination, and the more robust vices, were appeased, not by amendment of life, but by penances, servility to the monks, and an abject and illiberal devotion." Would that virtuous man have written the next following lines, if he had known, that his ashes would have been cursed by zealots? "Though most men, anywise eminent, have found reason to complain of calumny, I never was touched," says he, "or even attacked, by her baleful tooth; and though I wantonly exposed myself to the rage of both civil, and religious factions, they seemed to be disarmed, in my behalf, of their wonted fury. My friends never had occasion to vindicate any one circumstance of my character, and conduct: not but that the zealots, we may well suppose, would have been glad to invent, and propagate any story to my disadvantage, but they could never find any which they thought would wear the face of probability."

But, what is virtue? It is to bear up against adversities with calmness, and heroism; it is to gain our subsistence with honour among the vicious; virtue is to speak truth against our own interest; it is never to complain of the injustice of our fortune; virtue is the losing the opportunity of acquiring glory when we are wanting in another part for the good of our fellow-creatures; virtue is a constant endeavour to better our own character: In a word, virtue is nothing else than a divine goodness of humanity. If you love letters, you have nothing to do, but to aim at the perfection of your own character: your book is your own heart;

and in whatever situation you might be, in comparing yourself with others, avoid all their faults, imitate all their fine qualities, and your eloquence will touch every heart.

LORENZO.

TO CHARLES.

New York.

Virtue is a quality much more rare than is generally imagined; and therefore the words humanity, virtue, patriotism, and many others of similar kinds, should be used with greater caution than they usually are in the intercourses of mankind.

Zimmerman.

Those, who are taught by their philosophy, properly to estimate the merits of every people, will feel disgust when they hear persons inveighing against a nation for the sole purpose of indirectly boasting, that their own country is free from the defects which they censure. I was once introduced by an American family to a French lady. After she had sung several patriotic songs, I conversed with her in her native tongue. As the French language was not understood by the rest of the company, she lavished praises upon the French nation in so outrageous a manner, that it seemed, according to her judgment, that all others were deficient. As she was not informed, upon my introduction to her, that I was an Italian, I thought it my duty to tell her that I was not a native of France. I proceeded as follows: As I have kind, delicate, and sensible friends among the French people, I have the honour to tell you, Madam, that I love them as my own. I am one of those cosmopolites, who believe, that a person has no right to disregard a nation, because he observes in it, particular instances of depravity, for, he should reflect, that man is always man with more, or less modification, according to the age in which he lives. We cannot find a single nation which is not adorned by men of virtue, and my impression is, that we are prejudiced in favour of our native country, because we there received the first caresses of our parents. Upon this, perhaps too severe reproof, she assumed the expression of a cunning fox, and, had I been Raphael, I would have given to the world a singular, and striking picture. However we proceeded to converse on various topics; and the subject of languages rising, I advanced the proposition, that no language is perfect, since we find, that in all those with which we are acquainted, there are many words wanting to express our sentiments. "You must possess a great genius, sir," said she, with her cunning smile, "since the languages spoken by nations through so long a course of years, are insufficient to give expression to your ideas." I was not unprepared for this exhibition of petty revenge. Poor humanity! We seem born to make painful the lives of each other. Sometimes I endeavor to explain to myself the inequality of the gifts of nature. In the very moment that she delights to bestow upon one all the good qualities of mind and body, she inflicts upon another, external deformity joined with a repulsive character. Why, I ask myself, are we not all cast in the same mould? One is blind, another lame, the face of this is turned upon his left shoulder, and that bears it on his right. This man jumps on crutches, and that sees nothing deserving attention except his own precious person: the one is passionate, the other sardonic. This man is a fool, and that delights to insult him with his clownish wit.... But, I have entered into too long a digression: so that, resuming the thread of the conversation, although I like to yield to the ladies, I was not disposed to give the victory to her.

> "It is the witness still of excellency
> To put a strange face on his own perfection,"

Says Shakespeare. So that, wishing to put all my poor wit into operation, Madam, said I, I do not believe myself to be a genius because I cannot name with a particular word every part compounding this chair which I now hold. Besides, ifI were in love with you, Madam, I do not believe that I should find words adequate to the description of your charms, as Byron says:

> "Who hath not proved how feebly words essay
> To fix one spark of beauty's heavenly ray?"

And Chateaubriand: "Ah, si tu m'aimais, quelle, serait notre félicité! Nous trouverions pour nous exprimer un langage digne du ciel; à présent il y a des mots qui manquent, parce que ton âme ne répond pas à la mienne."

She smiled with her natural cheerfulness, and we continue now to be good friends.

LORENZO.

TO LORENZO.

London.

Those, who find themselves severed from society by peculiarities of form, if they do not hate the common bulk of mankind, are at least not altogether indisposed to enjoy their mishaps, and calamities.   *Walter Scott.*

Though we say, man ought not to be partial to his own country, still we find a great many travellers judging of

nations with rashness. The prejudices of our childhood are
so dangerous to our reason, that very often men endeavour
to find faults among nations, because they have not their
own habits. A traveller may converse with thousands of individuals of a foreign nation which he undertakes to describe, and still, have no idea of their real character. We
have   only to open their books, and we find nothing is so
full of contradictions as the   writers on their journeys.
From whence does it come, that Madam Destaël praises so
much the Italian nation, whilst Lady Morgan debases
them, if it is not, that Destaël had the good chance of finding among them something agreeable to her, and Morgan
displeasing things? Besides, the life of a man is hardly sufficient for   judging of a nation, since, admitting he under-
stands the language, if on many an occasion we find the
character of particular persons very different from what
we   have judged before, so, with greater reason, we may
mistake the character of a whole nation. In the first period
of his residence in Italy, Byron judged of the Italians in a
quite different manner from what he did, during the last
period of his   life. Who can read Alfieri's Misogallo without feeling the injustice of his having written so contemp-
tuously of the nation of Fenelon, Mably, Montesquieu, and
so on? How can we find justice among men, if eminent
writers depreciate other nations with rashness? In opening
a book of Madam Destaël, and reading several praises on
Italy, I find the following lines: "In that nation, where one
does not think but love, there is not a single romance, because love is so rapid, so public, that it yields no develop-
ment: and to pen with reality the general manners on this
subject, it would be necessary to begin, and finish in the
first page." There are authors, who sometimes prefer to
show their wit at the expense of their good sense, since

Madam Destaël knowing the life of Dante, Petrarch, Tasso, and many other Italians, she could not deny that, although Italy has not so great a quantity of romances in prose as the French library, still she has persons of both sexes, whose life was only a long chain of Platonic love. However a romance is only but a plot on which love acts the first part: and if it is so, how can we agree with Madam Destaël for the mere reason the Italian writers had chosen other subjects? But, still, the form implies nothing if the substance is the same: so, if France has romances written in prose, Italy has as many Italian romances in poetry. If every writer, who undertakes to speak badly of some nations have the following just sentiment of Chateaubriand, we would have the satisfaction of not meeting with so much nonsense: "Malgé les nombreuses injustices que Chactas avait eprouvées de la part des Français, il les aimait. Il se sovenait toujours de Fénélon, dont il avait été l'hôte, et désirait pouvoir rendre quelque service aux compatriotes de cet homme vertueux." We know, that Chateaubriand had been the guest of Washington.

CHARLES.

TO LORENZO.

Lausanne.

O ruines! je retournerai vers vous prendre vos leçons! je me replacerai dans la paix de vos solitudes; et là, éloigné du spectacle affligeant des passions, j'aimerai les hommes sur des souvenirs; je m'occuperai de leur bonheur, et le mien se composera de l'idée de l'avoir hâté. *Volney.*

Every thing is now in bloom; and that snow on which I rode on a sledge two months ago has disappeared. In the short space of a century, all these mortals contending for a span of ground will have vanished in the same manner: but, time has no power when history relates to posterity the good, or bad qualities of men.

Yes, I have propensity to think with you. We, perhaps, a small part of the Soul animating the whole creation, are not happy, unless we find a Being able to partake our sentiments.

Compose for me, Lorenzo, a sonnet on the Sepulchre of Santarosa.

OONALASKA.

TO CHARLES.

Richmond.

For what end has the lavish hand of Providence diffused innumerable objects of delight, but that all might rejoice in the privilege of existence, and be filled with gratitude to the beneficent author of it. *Carter.*

If it were given to me the enjoyment of the love that men attempt to snatch from my grasp; and afterwards, provided I were leaving beyond my grave no stain injuring my honour, I would die without regret, though I was sure that my spirit would pass into a state of nonentity. Life seems but an ephemeral moment between the infinite passed time and the next to come: so, being it the centre of two infinite extremities, the world must be the beginning, and end for every mortal Being: but, I think this universe has always been, and it will never be destroyed. I believe it is Voltaire, who said: "Nous sommes d'hier, et l'Amérique est de ce matin."

I saw Oonalaska in a dream with all the attractions of her charms! The world now seems to me the garden of Armida. How beautiful, Charles, is the ruin on that mountain! That lightning striking just now the top of that tree, it does not present to my mind tyranny and despotism: I see nothing else in it, but nature falling at the feet of Oonalaska, and worshiping her beauty. Sun of this fine universe; when thou wilt glitter in vain for me, do, tell her, though I was without hope of meeting her on earth, when in my life I turned out of the way of her virtuous sentiments, it was my ignorance of not being able to discern my duty; never willingly!

To-day I read "Gerusalemme Liberata," which had never been delivered from the hands of the Turk into another called the Pope. Misfortune was the inheritance of Tasso. Passions, and sufferings seem the only movers of that genius. In reading the episode of Olindo and Sofronia, I was thinking of the writer's walking with agitation in his room, suffused with tears, stopping from time to time, and speaking to Eleonora as if she were present. But, suddenly, with eyes cast down, almost breathless, taking the pen, inspired by a divinity, smiling with a tear ready to drop on the paper, and writing these fine lines:

> "O sia grazia del ciel che l'umiltade
> D'innocente pastor salvi, e sublime,

O che siccome il folgore non cade
In basso pian, ma su l'eccelse cime:
Casi il furor di peregrine spade
Sol de' gran re l'altere teste oprime:
Ne gli avidi soldati a preda alletta
La nostra povertà vile e negletta."

What shame for those, who made him pass for a fool!
Once, a friend of mine, speaking about geniuses, thought
the pre-occupation, or concentrating state in which sometimes a man of talent dives, appears something near to
foolishness. A man starting from a profound meditation,
seems as one awaking from sleep by a sudden noise; and
wishing to speak before his clear ideas be at his command, all he is saying is nothing but absurdities. Reflection having no part in his discourse, a man of a great
mind is more apt to talk foolishness, than a real fool.

Yesterday walking in a dale, I found William sitting
on a rock in gloomy meditation. "I am, Lorenzo," said
he, "like a terrestrial bird in the middle of an immense
sea, flying in search of land with exhausted wings: but,
the more it looks around the wild horizon, the more its
piercing eye discovers the flood interminable, and black
clouds, forwarded by lightning, hovering over its head...
After a long pause. — Society, he proceeded, is for me the
same dreadful ocean? I killed by a vain point of honour
the brother of Julia in a duel. When I saw my dearest
friend struggling with death, putting my homicidal
hand on the wound, I swore to use arms no more."

To-day I read an account of a dreadful execution under the tyrannical laws of Don Miguel:[13] the priests of
Christ, after having led to the scaffold seven young men,
whose crime was that of having tried the liberty of their
country, and getting rid of such a monster, those very

ministers, who durst to speak with the moral of Jesus, were afterwards praying in church for the preservation of the tyrant of Portugal.

Please to send the following Sonnet to Oonalaska.

IL SEPOLCRO DI SANTAROSA.

Sonetto.

Il fumo che sboccò da tutte l'armi,
    Formava in Grecia grande mausoleo:
    Cangiando sull'Ausonia in un trofeo,
    Qual nuovo Sole il vidi innanzi starmi.
Tre Dive usciro tra funebri canni,
    Scendendo il frale sul colle Euganeo,
    Vè già Natura ombrosa grotta feo,
    E dorme l'Ortis sotto i freddi marmi.
Ma l'ombra di Canova ch'era accanto
    Del suo lavoro al monumento bello,
    Baciollo, e l'irrorò di caldo pianto.
Raccolto poscia lo divin scalpello,
    Di Caritade incise il voler santo:
    "Il Cielo a Santarosa erse l'avello.

LORENZO.

————————————————

TO OONALASKA.

New-York.

It is only through woe that we are taught to reflect, and we gather the honey of worldly wisdom, not from flowers, but thorns.   *Bulwer.*

When I find a man continually at variance with himself, it is with difficulty, that I hinder myself from smiling bitterly, thinking, that at the very moment in which he is searching for a comfortable life, and supposing himself in possession of a harbour, the waves swallow him forever, and lies a miserable wreck. A young lady loses her mother: the silent pains of her heart, prevent the free course of her tears: at length she cries and laughs at the same time: and whilst mourning over the wretchedness of mortal life, we meet with a malicious, conceited, and small minded woman, who, because you did not pay her the vile baseness of a courtier, the next time you have the politeness to pay her a visit, she will either not be at home, sick, or not able to return your kindness in consequence of the indisposition of her child: and though she goes to church, and believes nobody saved out of her creed, she will be very much pleased after such wickedness, and showing superiority towards her fellow creature. Do you know why? Her boasted religion is not her ruling passion; it is that of despotism. So, when nature spares us from pains, whilst we complain of the wretchedness of our life, we endeavor to torment each other.

There is no reality on this little globe, and sometimes I desire its destruction by coming in contact with some other planets, perhaps worse than this, and bury in a moment our shameful race in which the most cunning triumph over the just. So Byron:

> "Some men are worms
> In soul more than the living things of tombs."

I have too strong a conviction of the perfection of astronomy for believing a comet might destroy the fine order of it: but, when my imagination, and mankind's perversity exalt my mind, I think with some passages of the Bible, that God cannot be satisfied with our ill-nature. The spectacle of the destruction of this globe, must be a very agreeable, and sublime moment for the virtuous man, who did not find but ingratitude: it is not the spirit of vengeance; it is the pleasure of seeing the end of a planet, in which the best is very often doomed to suffer under the paw of the most cunning animal. Yesterday I felt in my heart the nails of a falcon hovering over me, when my ears were pierced by the dying screams of an innocent bird under its talons.

I hear great many complaining of the ingratitude which man meets with man: but, if they examine their own conscience with equity, they should find, that while they feel the blows they have received, forget the mortal ones they gave unjustly to their fellow creatures. We have no right to reprehend our injuries, unless our conduct towards others be unblemished. The slightest slip from morality is enough to create thousand disorders in society: and if we were not overruled by the benevolent, and provident nature, the external order of society would have no more allurement for us. The most well disposed man if he is not an angel, by dint of finding himself the victim of his goodness, drinks with it a poison decaying his fine natural qualities; so that, in answering blow for blow, soon finds himself dragged to the level of the very scoundrels, whom at first he was so reluctant to be associated with. So the few aristocrats have their complaints because they cannot tyrannize the plurality: the latter by want of instruction, not being able to revenge their real sufferings, imitate the former upon those, who feel a second rank of inferiority, and so on, one spoil another until that the most abject class of men, by want of finding other inferior of them, when the last spark of moral becomes extinguished in their heart, finding themselves contemned by society, they finish always by giving themselves to crimes, for whom, lawyers have a good opportunity of demonstrating, that, if it happens to find briberies protecting the rascalities of the rich; at least they have laws always exact, and severe, in judging the rabble. So Shakespeare: "The Worser allow'd by order of law a furr'd gown to keep him warm; and furr'd with fox and lamb skins too, to signify, that craft, being richer than innocency, stands for the facing." In our present state of society, the man's existence is only a lottery. Society not only do not help the poor; but, every individual turns the back to a man, who has nothing in the world. Bugiardo has some bad goods to sell; and if he does not gain money with it, he must perish: so, he will tell the lie to save himself on such only plank. How can we call society a compound of bustling human creatures, leaving the poor struggling with necessity, when in helping him, it would turn not only on his favour, but on the happiness of the whole commonwealth? In a country like this, wanting population, we find suicides as frequent as in Europe. This country, Oonalaska, though, at my notion, is the most promising throughout the world, still she wants better administration. Yesterday, passing by Maidenlane, seeing a track of blood crossing the street, I went to a crowd surrounding the dead body of a merchant, who cut his throat when he found himself failed in his business.

For what reason Machiavelli the teacher of Buonaparte, has not the thousandth part of admirers of his pupil, if it were not by having taken no advantage with depriving society of her rights, and turning it into his favour by the superiority of his mind? A musician becomes rich by the exertion of his art; and people will not only prefer him to a philosopher, whose reason improves their own happiness; but, their blind ignorance will force them to call such a philanthropist an exalted man, or a fool. Human praises spring from success, not from real intrinsic merit: and "I patimenti dei grandi uomini formano la felicità del genere umano."

A day after another leads us where? Indeed I do not know: but, if we come on this earth only to kick and cuff each other, what kind of existence is ours, if not a pestiferous exhalation of hell, leaving, behind its paths, indelible traces of death? When we shall lie in the common abode of lethargy from whence we came to this life, our past, painful, or delightful existence will be alike for us: but, some in reality, and some by imagination, we may say, few have the fortune to call this earth an Eden. We are sociable creatures by selfishness: and still, what kind of sociability, if continually in guard one against another? Then silence, while it seems proceeding from a want of confidence, it is because we fear to lose our respectability in the sight of fellows always ready to take advantage on the goodness, and innocent abandonment of another.

If nature were giving us in a moment a sense bringing into light our secret thoughts, few would stay in public without shame. However, sciences and arts going on, whilst are purifying the human heart, are always clearing the clouds of ignorance, superstition, and hypocrisy, three evils leading mankind into such a hellish confusion, that man thinks foolishness to follow integrity. But, they may chain Prometheus on the top of Caucasus, and leave him the prey of ravens; they may forsake Columbus begging bread for his son; cast Galileo into a dungeon, and leave Thomas Paine dying on the straw: but, people will always learn, that Jupiter was a tyrant, the Scripture's writers less mathematicians than Columbus, that the earth turns around the sun, and Paine a true citizen.

The love of ourselves being a natural instinct for our conservation, it should be the mover of all fine actions, if it were based on true principles of society. But, it is painful for those, who, knowing the source of inex-hausted pleasures, that the human compact might pos-sess, see at the same time the impossibility to reach it among flocks of ignorants. Improvements rose but with our reason; and our interest turns on our loss, when it is not bound with the happiness of the whole mankind. This common interest is what wise men call love of true glory.

Though our social improvements are too slow for the suffering virtue, still, we are always going a step towards perfection. From the fall of a nation, another learns, and be-comes wiser: this falls, the other rises: but, history stands there a monument of light which is only offending the sight of owls, and bats. It will come the day in which every man finding his own interest on the way of integrity, the selfish eloquence of rascals will be scorned, and trampled by an enlightened people. It is with sorrow of mind I find among Americans too much anxiety of money. If this wise govern-ment were encouraging superior men on every side of the United States to deliver public lectures on history, showing to the people the evil of the times which are past, America would become the polestar of a true Republic. All she wants now, it is instruction.

Who would have believed, before the invention of ves-sels, that man would have sailed around the globe? And now, who would believe our age or posterity will find the means of swimming in the air? Till now the attempts of go-ing against the wind have failed: but, if I were a mechanic, I would construe a balloon in the shape of a fish; and by means of a machine, I would move the fins in several di-rections. It seems to me it would not be difficult to swim against the airy element as the fishes do against the most rapid waterfalls.

Yes, you are right, Oonalaska; in private life, very seldom a man can judge another, our feelings being so dispar-
ate as the sound of human voices: still, if every sensible
man were obliged to answer at every displeasure he meets
in society, he should be obliged to use very often the
sword, or pistol. We are always in contradiction by want of
understanding. Once, I was praising with Catholics the virtue of Brutus when he supported with heroism the death
of his sons: and such Christians, who could not compre-
hend and thought unnatural a father condemning his children to death, sustained with all their energy that hereafter
we might see in hell our father, mother, sons, and wife
without the least pain, if God have condemned them. I find
in the Alcoran the same stoicism. "O croyans! cessez d'aimer vos pères, vos frères s'ils préfèrent l'incrédulite à la
fois. Si vous les aimez, vous deviendrez pervers. Si vos
pères, vos enfans, vos freres, vos epouses, vos parens, les
richesses que vous avez acquises, le commerce dont vous
craignez la ruine, vos habitations chéries ont plus d'empire
sur vos cœurs que Dieu, son envoyé, et la guerre sainte, at-
tendez le jugement du Très-Haut."

P. S. Bran my only, and faithful companion of my misfortune is so much attached to me, that I find no language
apt to explain this dog's feeling. Whilst I write this letter,
his head is on my knees. The sagacity of this animal is beyond comprehension. I heard always this dog growling
every time a man, whom I thought honest, came in my
room; I heard afterwards he is a swindler, and cheated me
out of twenty dollars.

I went to pay a visit to the tomb of my friend C..... I put
a wreath of perpetual flowers on his modest cross, bearing
his name, and made a little garden on the small piece of
ground covering his remain. But, whilst I was engaged in

such a pious ceremony, my eyes did neither contemplate the immense void of the skies, nor I did think of my infancy's feeble prayers. His lively existence is gone like a river, which receives motion by dashing against rocks on a declivity. Enjoyments, and sorrows were the rocks which gave him existence, until he found in the vale of death a monotonous silence.

Yes, Oonalaska, Ada was not only beautiful; but, the qualities of her mind were such, that you would have found in her a sincere friend. Far from being, as often we see silly girls, full of presumption, always pleased whenever they can show before the object of their thoughts, that their religion does not go so far as to correct their uncivil carelessness towards the politeness of a friendless gentleman. Her disposition was retiring, and conciliatory. In her whole life she never committed intentionally a single unkind deed, or thought towards her fellow being. When, by distraction, Ada believed she had not reciprocated the attentions of those around her, she was thoughtful, and mortified; but reconciliation immediately illumined her divine countenance with joy, and gratification. One day, Ada, Charles, and myself having proposed to go on the top of a mountain, not far from her father's house, Charles finding Ada on the out door, offered her his arm. Though she wanted to be with me, her gentility did not permit her to refuse the mere politeness of Charles. On reaching the top of the mountain, we found a Chapel surrounded of tombs, and under the altar, the grave of her younger sister, which she drew my attention to, with tears rolling down her cheeks. She kneeled down, and prayed so fervently, that I was prompted to do the same. On rising, she took my hand, and led me silently to the ground fresh moved, in which lay one of my friends, a few days before deceased, over which our aspirations commingled! And now, where is Ada?—In the grave with her sister! Few know that sacred place, and perhaps nobody has now a friendly recollection of Ada. I passed one night on her cold tombstone; and I felt her spirit hovering around me, and caressing my forehead.—I heard the angelic sound of her voice; and told in my ear, that I would have been unhappy all my life, because I dare to speak truth among men unable of understanding me. Never mind, Oonalaska, now that the sufferings became my element, as I think with the following lines of Chateaubriand, let the prophecy of Ada be fulfilled: "Mais qu'importent la mort, et les revers, si notre nom, prononcé dans la postérité, va faire battre un cœur généreux deux mille ans après notre vie?"

You are one of those angels, Oonalaska, that God sends from time to time to teach us we are sons of heaven. All professors of Divinity may say every thing they will on the wickedness of mankind: but, around the worthy, I breathe an embalmed air which opens my heart, and then I am not ashamed to be a man.

LORENZO.

TO CHARLES.
New-York.

Non nihil aspersis gaudet amor lacrymis.

All fine qualities were united in her. She was reading on a chair near the window, from which is seen the fine prospect of a chain of mountains losing itself in the clouds, and at the right, undulating hills, which, decreasing with the distance, terminate in a vast plain, the ending of which, is the shore of an interminable sea. Her hair was veiling her dazzling countenance; and the tears dropping from her large eyes, were like the morning dews on the queen of flowers. O, why did I not breathe that sweet sigh which embalmed the air with heavenly fragrance? And to whom was directed her sigh!... Her heart is formed to feel for sufferers. I shall recollect all my life when she spoke with those, who were detracting the character of poor Henry, her words sound yet in my heart. "Genius is banished," she said, "where luxury is introduced; and love is a chimera where merit is not appreciated. By a certain impulse, natural to us, we join house to house: but selfishness makes divisions between us. Man lives with man, not by having his character assimilated to his own; but, because fortune permitted him to have the same quantity of servants. Look on the people of Geneva, whilst they call themselves republicans, they are not ashamed to repeat the aristocratical phrase: 'Gens du haut.' Every body endeavours to obtain the rich man's friendship for no other motive than that of having his consideration, which, as they believe, it may turn in favour of their increasing property: but, they do not think they are gathering flowers on a precipice, instead of taking them on an even meadow." Angel of my suffering heart, excuse if I tremble for thy virtue; but, how can I be calm, whilst thy boat is passing between Scylla, and Charybdis?

Charles, when I think on thy friendship, on the pure love of Oonalaska, and the tender affection of my family, no, I cannot be unhappy. The morning walk with Oonalaska near Lausanne, is always in my imagination.

Leaving our company behind, we reached the top of the hill; She was leaning on my arm shaded with her hair, which like a black veil hanged loosened on her shoulders: her left hand was in mine; and silently waiting the rising sun, her large eyes were steadily fixed on the morning star. My God, if the enjoyments of blissful regions are not like the pleasure I felt in her lovely tears, let me live a single year in the rapturous delight of her love, and I renounce forever to the heavenly immortality of my soul. After so great a favour, shall I ask of thee an endless happiness! Whenever I think of her I feel this life of cares, difficulties, and adversities, changed into a delightful Eden; and everything smiling around me. How, Almighty, without Oonalaska would I be able to admire thy greatness, and worship thy glory! She is the image of thy Divinity. In her, I feel the love of my God; and when forlorn I think to the solitary place, now consecrated with her tears, I often find myself involuntarily on my knees adoring the Creator. When I feel in my dreams her rosy lips pressing my mouth, suddenly it awakes me, and I feel the existence of a God.

LORENZO.

From the above letters with some unconnected thoughts of our hero, we argue, that, though he avoid to speak of himself, his life having been tossed by great many misfortunes it would afford great interest if related. He migrated almost around the world; and when he heard Mr Ethelbert's family went to England, he returned to Switzerland among his old acquaintances.

He used to board in a house, where the pretty daughter of the landlady when had either said Walter Scott, Byron, Madam Cottin, or Destaël are fine writers, she thought it was enough to show the acuteness of her intellect: and whilst everybody admired the volubility of her tongue in praising such, and such preacher, she did never lose the opportunity of presenting Lorenzo, when absent, with manners injuring his reputation, because when Lorenzo was at the dinner table, he was sometimes so much abstracted, that he forgot all petty attentions which a gentleman is often compel to use. Her mother's conversation would have tired the most benevolent hearer with her incessant praises about her daughter: a fop, who believed all ladies were in love with his pretty long person, and ten thousand livres a year; and a widower, who wanting to get a young wife to give instruction to his large daughters, whose discourse, when his sweet-heart was present, rolled on his bravery, and his ability of shooting a fox at the distance of two hundred yards, were all the boarders, besides Lorenzo, of that fashionable house. But, as our hero was silent, and thoughtful, he did not mind such self conceited creatures sneering on his back.

One of the most uncharitable sin of human society, it will always be the pleasure of the envious disregarding the absent. The superiority of Lorenzo was such, that persons of small education could put no price on his fine qualities: and, though they could not deny his superiority when he was present, in the long course of his absence, several malevolent creatures prevailed in such a manner against him, that in arriving thither, even great many of his friends received him with coolness, and indifference.

One evening Lorenzo being in a large circle of ladies, and gentlemen, Mr Hugo, the very one, as we have related, whom was knocked down by our hero when they were school boys, was speaking of Mr Ethelbert, as an Englishman unworthy his country by having sentiments against liberty. Lorenzo, who was speaking with a young lady, intimate friend of Oonalaska, hearing to disregard her father, could not forbear from remarking to the detractor, that what seemed to Mr Hugo deserving reprobation, would perhaps be for Mr Ethelbert the most meritorious, and good intention towards his country.

"You would not defend Mr Ethelbert, sir; if you were not in love with his daughter."

"Your answer, sir, deserves to be reproved, since, suppose I love Miss Oonalaska, it is not your inspection to publish it. But, if I defend Mr Ethelbert, it might be either for the love of his daughter, or for the propensity of defending an absent gentleman."

"You speak like a brave man, Mr Lorenzo; but, we know very well, that if you were so, when we were boys, your character has changed a great deal in your manhood."

"It is, perhaps, such a conviction which gives you boldness. Did you ever read Spurzheim?"[14]

"Yes, sir; but, though your skull announces a man of genius, I would not stick for your courage."

"It is the first time, sir, I hear praising my skull. But, in answer to your doubting of my courage, I would say, it is a hard matter to judge one's courage. I do not know if the theory of Spurzheim is a good one to judge human character: but, whatever it may be, I find in his books many things deserving the attention of those, who want study human nature. He says, there are different combinations of causes, which form the character of man: for instance, we cannot say that man is wanting courage, because in many an occasion he acted with prudence. The protuberance indicating courage being larger than anybody else: but, that of benevolence being superior, he will always check his self-esteem, when he finds himself on the way of being a murderer."

"Your language is that of a coward defending his pusillanimity: but, since your benevolence checks your self-esteem, I may say, without danger, before these ladies, and gentlemen, that Mr Ethelbert is a scoundrel, as well as any body wishing to protect him."

"Whilst you name ladies, and gentlemen, sir, you bring to my recollection that, as I am before a respectable company, I, cannot use your mean expressions."

Lorenzo withdrew; and on the next morning the following letter was sent:

TO HUGO.

Geneva.

I have marked a brave spirit succeed in buffeting its way out of its adversities; and I have seen as brave a one overcome by them, and falling vanquished, even with the sword of resolution gleaming in its grasp; for there are combinations of evil against which no human energies can make a stand.

The Diary of a late Physician.

If it were not my duty to defend an absent friend of mine, who would not pass an insult unrevenged, your conduct being contemptible, for my own part, I think it deserves not my resentment. — You are under obligation to retract your slander, and acknowledge before the same society, that Mr Ethelbert is a gentleman of respect, and esteem, otherwise you know very well, that your language of yesterday evening deserves no benevolence towards you.

LORENZO.

TO LORENZO.

Geneva.

To-morrow morning at 6 o'clock I am at Ferney's tavern to your invitation with a brace of pistols, which we must discharge at the distance of pocket handkerchief.

HUGO.

TO LORENZO.

Geneva.

Yesterday evening I wanted to leave the society with you: but, I thought proper to stay, and prevent any further slander. Robinson, the American gentleman, spoke a long time in your favour, and said, nobody would call Lorenzo a coward, if he had seen you as he did, when you jumped in the middle of New-York's bay to rescue a boy, who fell in the water, and bring him with difficulty on the shore.

To-day I heard great many reproaching the behaviour of Hugo: he could not find here a single person willing to be his stickler. The whole town turned him the back.

GARNERI.

————————————————

TO CHARLES.

Geneva.

Hearing you are in Saint-Etienne, I hurry you this letter.—I am dragged to a duel with Hugo, and want you in Ferney to-morrow morning at 6 o'clock.

LORENZO.

Charles received the letter of his friend in the evening, mounted immediately his horse, and went to Geneva. In reaching the house, he asked the landlady information of Lorenzo.

"He is just gone to bed, said she: the servant told me he wrote letters all the evening."

Charles went to his bed-room; and finding his friend in a quiet slumber, sat next his bed, and signed the servant to go without noise. At day-break the carriages through the streets, awaked our hero, who found his dear Charles by him.

"Charles, how long since are you here?"

At his voice, Charles embraced Lorenzo without uttering a syllable.

"Have you any news of my sisters, and brothers, Charles?"

"Yes, they are all well."

"God bless them. When I shall be no more, give them those letters I left on that table. See from the window what kind of weather is it."

"It is very damp."

"What hour is it?"

"Five o'clock."

"Let us go out. Did you come on horseback?"

"Yes."

"Well, Charles, let us ride to Ferney."

In a moment they got on their horses: and before reaching Coutance, they stopped a little on the bridge.

"Before this blue water, Charles, will have reached Bellegarde, where loses itself under the rocks for some while, I shall have ceased thinking of Oonalaska, and the hope at once of seeing her again. Death should be nothing for me, if she were not in this side of the grave."

"That scoundrel ought to fight with me before. When we were boys he would have beat me to death without your interference. Besides, Ethelbert not only is one of my countrymen; but, he was a friend of mine before you were acquainted with him."

"I would not have called you, if your intention is to broil yourself with my antagonist. — If you do not promise me your coolness, and after my death to renounce any hatred against him, let me go alone."

"But, Lorenzo!"

"No, Charles, I insist. I would die unhappy if you do not promise me to take no revenge after me."

"Well, I shall not displease you!"

They were now out of the gate of the city, and Lorenzo indicating Les Paquis,

"There, said he to his friend, Oonalaska gave me this ring. When they will bury me, let nobody take it off from my finger. It is the promise of our unfortunate love. You will find Bran chained in the stable: it is a present of Oonalaska to me, which now I make a present to you, Charles: he is one of the largest dogs I have seen. I thought proper not to take him with us, because if he sees me falling on the ground, he would eat my antagonist."

They reached Ferney; and did not stay a quarter of an hour in the tavern, when Hugo with a certain Rolland came in; and without uttering a word to Lorenzo, or Charles, Hugo swallowed up a full glass of pure brandy which, as it seemed, was not the first he had drunk in that awful morning. Rolland in going out with Hugo, told their antagonists they were going in the wood.

"Will you take any stimulant, Lorenzo?" "No, my dear."

"Though I do believe that wretch is tired of his life, I saw in a corner of his eyes, that he does not face death as he pretended: and, I do opine, if he were not drunk, he would retract."

They followed their antagonists. It was quite a sublime, and awful moment in seeing the heart-aching pains of Charles graved on his manly and noble countenance, whilst the smooth, calm, firm, and cheerful Lorenzo was endeavouring to cheer his friend with his sound reason. In seeing the interest of those two noble friends they had for each other, you would have thought it was Charles, who was going to death; not Lorenzo. It is always on the brink of danger, that a great man shows the sublimity of his mind. At first he is careful, and prudent: but, when the step is done, he stands like a rock. In reaching their adversaries, Charles said to Rolland, that he was not come into such a place to be a spectator of a decided murder, and wanted to put them at the distance of chance.

"No, sir, uttered Hugo with the accent of a drunkard: the only chance is the snapping of the pistols. But I took all precautions to prevent it."

"Charles, said Lorenzo, do recollect your promise."

The mouths of their pistols were almost touching the breast of each other. A striking contrast was in the faces of the two antagonists: terror, hatred, and despair was printed in that of Hugo; whilst in Lorenzo's it was a heavenly serenity of pure conscience; he looked like an Angel fighting with Satan. At the command of three, the only pistol of Hugo was fired: and 'Lorenzo still holding his cocked pistol in his hand, fell in the arms of Charles.

"Charles, prevent the news of my death to be referred to Oonalaska.... If, in spite of your friendly interference, it will reach her ear, tell her, that in dying by such a death, contrary to her, and my principles, I did never have the less sentiment to murder my adversary, and that I want no other blessing but her forgiveness. Farewell, dear Charles!"

His pistol dropped; and, in shaking the hand of his friend, he expired with a smile on his lips. Among the letters he wrote the evening before, we shall produce the following, which Charles sent to Hugo.

TO CHARLES.

Geneva.

I thought it was a sad life, when we must be always obliged to be killing our fellow-creatures to preserve ourselves; and indeed, I think so still, and I would even now, suffer a great deal, rather than I would take away the life even of the worst person injuring me. I believe, also, all considering people,who know the value of life, would be of my opinion, if they entered seriously into the consideration of it.

Daniel De Foe.

Whilst you read this letter, the world has no more allurements for me: and the fire of the illustrious geniuses, and philosophers can warm my heart no more. I leave on this earth an object, which the whole world is nothing in comparison; an Angel; my Love; Oonalaska behind me! But, if I do not follow the plurality's sentiment, I should be considered a coward; and then, what kind of existence would be mine, I, whom am dependent from society? Indeed, it is very wrong to judge the courage of a man with so an unreasonable, and bad action. Dear Charles, I disapprove what society compels me to do. But, I have nothing, nothing on earth now but my honour! ... He slandered the father of Oonalaska…. Well; since my moral defends me to be a murderer, you will find my pistol loaded, by me: he is a wretch; but, he has a family; he must live for her sake. If we have another existence after this miserable one, and my example can touch his conscience, by leaving him time to become better, it might be still a place in heaven for him. If you wish bless my grave on this strange country, do not revenge the blood of your friend.

LORENZO!

TO CHARLES.

Geneva.

Il n'y a point de haine qu'on ne désarme a force de douceur, et de bans procédés; au lieu qu'au contraire la haine des méchans ne fait que s'animer davantage par l'impossibilité de trouver sur quoi la fonder.   *J. J. Rousseau.*

The magnanimity of Lorenzo, sir, touches me in so a delicate part of my heart, that I should be the most wretched creature on earth, if I do not confess to all the world a crime which is buried in my bosom. As you were the most intimate friend of Lorenzo, it is useless to tell you, sir, that I have killed the most virtuous young man: still, you do not know all the deeds of Lorenzo! I would not finish, if I were to relate you, the heroic actions of Lorenzo at my only notice: and though I accused my worthy countryman of cowardice, as I did see him in Italy to behave himself like a hero in the most difficult occasions, I did never have the less sensation of doubting his bravery. But, since I deprived society of so useful a member, my confession, will stop, at least, so many badly grounded braveries of duel.

Though, sir, I was challenged by Lorenzo, it is I, who drove so an honourable young man to such an excess. I loved Oonalaska; and finding myself refused, and her father not receiving my visits, at first I projected to kill Mr Ethelbert, and myself: but, thinking that so unnatural death would have stained, in the mind of the people, my recollection with horror, and detestation, I forced my rival Lorenzo to deliver me from a life which became every day most insupportable to me. God has punished me in sparing my miserable existence. But, if it will be given me to imitate a single virtue of Lorenzo, I will exert the greatest penance of my remaining days.

HUGO.

Charles after having put in order every thing of his friend, went back to Italy, and induced the brothers, and sisters of Lorenzo to settle in England. In reaching Calais, not being able to find Bran, Charles announced a high premium for any one, who would have brought his dog saved to him. After two months, Bran was found dead on the tomb-stone of Lorenzo, with a piece of his strong chain around his neck. By order of Charles, he was buried by Lorenzo's grave.

> E quelle parole frizzavano sull'anima della poveretta, come lo scorrere d'una mano ruvida sur una ferita.   *Manzoni.*[15]

All friendly attentions of Charles, could not prevent the terrible new from the ears of Oonalaska. For several days she could neither speak, eat, sleep, nor cry: her situation was the most dreadful. At length, she burst into laughing, and crying at a time: and after a year of silent sadness, and consumption we shall transcribe her last following words.

"O, my father, my father, Lorenzo died for you! Don't you see yonder? O, take away that bloody man! He is covered with the blood of Lorenzo. — Mother, this world is a very wretched one! — Lorenzo, in a few minutes, I am with you. Beyond that star, Lorenzo, no father has right to prevent me from being with you; beyond that star, no slanderer will be able to stain your reputation: the depravity, malignity, and envy of this human race is to be washed out: your integrity, your virtue, Lorenzo, will not only appear to the eyes of your Oonalaska; there, every one will see the excellence of your soul.—Father, mother, don't you see[16] that man dressed in black? His soul is black as his gown! He has endeavoured to stain the reputation of Lorenzo, whilst he called himself a minister of Christ. Father, if I spoke any unkind word to you, do, forgive your wretched child. Mother, you did never give me the less displeasure through whole my life. Father, mother, fare you well: don't cry for your only child! I am flying into the arms of Lorenzo: don't you see? He opens his arms to receive me! Do not cry! The affection of Lorenzo is that of a father, mother, brother, sister; he did never deceive me; he has always been kind to me; he is my best friend, my love."

She expired in the arms of her father, and mother, who seemed dying with her.

NOTES

[1] Markos Botsaris (1788-1823) was a Greek patriot and a celebrated hero of the Greek War of Independence (1821-1832).

[2] Santorre di Santarosa (1783-1825) was a leading figure of the Italian Risorgimento. He played a crucial role in the Piedmont revolution of 1821 which he chronicled in the book *De la révolution piémontaise*, published the same year. Forced into exile, he lived in Switzerland, France and England. In 1824, he volunteered for the Greek War of Independence and died in battle in 1825.

[3] An aria from Gioacchino Rossini's opera *La gazza ladra* (*The Thieving Magpie*), first performed in 1817.

[4] A line from the poem "Sei pur bella con gli astri sul crine" that Gabriele Rossetti (1783-1854), Italian patriot and father of Dante Gabriel and Christina Rossetti, published in 1820, on the occasion of the Neapolitan Revolution.

[5] Edward Bulwer-Lytton (1803-1873), British politician, poet, critic, and author of very popular historical novels, the best known of which is *The Last Days of Pompeii* (1834).

[6] Since Lorenzo's hometown is located in the region of Piedmont, it defies belief that a storm, however powerful, could have whisked away trees as far as the river Tiber, which rises on Monte Fumaiolo, between the central regions of Emilia Romagna and Tuscany and moves generally southward, finally flowing through the city of Rome and entering the Tyrrhenian Sea near Ostia. It is possible that Rocchietti mentioned the Tiber because of its name recognition and historical associations, or perhaps he simply had a tenuous grasp of Italy's geography, which was not uncommon, even among educated people, before the unification of the country.

[7] A quotation from the novel *The Vicar of Wakefield* (1766) by Oliver Goldsmith (1730-1774). As Carol Bonomo Albright and Elvira G. Di Fabio have noted, it is "not surprising that Rocchietti would have Lorenzo and Oonalaska reading *The Vicar of Wakefield* with its moral and social commentary on subjects dear to Rocchietti's heart" such as "freedom versus tyranny," "crime and punishment," "dignity and equality of all people," "familiar relations," "capital punishment," and "duelling" (Introduction 7).

8　A quotation from the novel *Guy Mannering or The Astrologer* (1815) by Sir Walter Scott (1771-1832). This was Scott's second Waverley novel, following the enormous success of *Waverley* (1814).

9　A quotation from *Delphine* (1802), the first novel by French-Swiss author Madame de Stäel (1766-1817). Like *Lorenzo and Oonalaska*, *Delphine* is written in epistolary form and ends with the tragic death of its protagonist (in her case, by suicide). Because of its unconventional protagonist, its reflections on the condition of women and its favorable references to British liberties, *Delphine* incurred the bitter disapproval of Napoleon Bonaparte and caused de Stäel to be exiled from Paris definitively.

10　A quotation from the comedy *L'argent* (1826) by popular French playwright Casimir Bonjour (1795-1856). Like Rocchietti, Bonjour was concerned about the growing prominence of money in modern society.

11　A quotation from *Ruines ou Méditations sur les révolutions des empires* (1791) by French philosopher, historian and orientalist Constantin-François de Chasseboeuf, count de Volney (1757-1820).

12　Filippo Pananti (1766-1837) was an Italian poet whose biography bears some resemblance to Rocchietti's. Pananti went into exile because his liberal ideas exposed him to danger in his native Tuscany. Afterwards, like Rocchietti, he made a living by teaching Italian and mathematics. His best-known work is arguably the autobiographical poem *Il poeta di teatro*, published in England in 1808, which shows the influence of Lawrence Sterne. Having decided to return to Italy in 1813, while on route from Calais to Sicily, Pananti was captured by Algerine pirates and held in captivity. After regaining his freedom, he lived in Algiers and explored North Africa while waiting for the opportunity to reach Sicily. He recounted his misadventure and his travels in the book *Avventure ed osservazioni sulle coste di Barberia* (1817) from which Rocchietti's quotation is taken.

13　Michael of Portugal (1802-1866) was the younger son of King John VI and briefly the regent of Portugal in February of 1828 before proclaiming himself king in July of the same year. However, his royal title was not universally recognized. A firm believer in the absolute rule of the monarch, once in power he launched a brutal persecution of his liberal adversaries.

[14] Johann Kaspar Spurzheim (1776–1832) was a German physician and one of the main proponents of phrenology.

[15] A quotation from Alessandro Manzoni's novel *I promessi sposi* (*The Betrothed*), first published in 1827.

[16] The one editorial intervention here is the addition of the word "see." It becomes clear as one reads this series of exhortations by Oonalaska, that the word "see" was missing from the original phrase, "Father, mother, don't you that man dressed in black?"

ABOUT THE AUTHOR

JOSEPH ROCCHIETTI, born in 1798 or 1799, was a native of Casale Monferrato, in Piedmont, Italy. He emigrated to the United States in 1830, possibly for political reasons, and made a living as a foreign language teacher. In 1835 he published what is regarded as the earliest Italian American novel, *Lorenzo and Oonalaska*. He followed it with the Italian-language tragedy *Ifigenia* (1842) and the pamphlet *Why a National Literature Cannot Flourish in the United States of North America* (1845) which, because of its provocative title, caught the attention of Edgar Allan Poe. His last known published work was the play *Charles Rovellini: A Drama of the Disunited States of North America* (1875), set during the Civil War. Rocchietti died in 1879.

ABOUT THE EDITOR

LEONARDO BUONOMO is Professor of American Literature at the University of Trieste, Italy. He is the author of three books: *Backward Glances: Exploring Italy, Reinterpreting America (1831-1866)* (1996); *From Pioneer to Nomad: Essays on Italian North American Writing* (2003); and *Immigration, Ethnicity, and Class in American Writing, 1830-1860* (2014). More recently he has published essays in the volumes *Nathaniel Hawthorne in Context* (2018) and *Republics and Empires: Italian and American Art in Transnational Perspective, 1840-1970* (2021), as well as in the journals *Nathaniel Hawthorne Review, Henry James Review, Ácoma, RSA Journal, Italian Americana, Humanities,* and has edited the volume *The Sound of James: The Aural Dimension in Henry James's Work* (2021). In 2019 he served as President of the Henry James Society.

SPUNTINI

This book series is dedicated to the long essay. It includes those studies that are longer than the traditional journal-length essay and yet shorter than the traditional book-length manuscript. Intellectually, it is a light meal, a snack of sorts that holds you over for the full helping that comes with either lunch or dinner.

Anthony Julian Tamburri. *The Columbus Affair: Imperatives for an Italian American Agenda.* Volume 1. ISBN 978-1-955995-00-9

Joseph Rocchietti. *Lorenzo and Oonalaska.* A Novel. Edited with an Introduction and Notes by Leonardo Buonomo. Volume 2. ISBN 978-1-955995-01-6

Lightning Source UK Ltd.
Milton Keynes UK
UKHW040652050922
408358UK00001B/270